THE EXCHANGE

Rachel Astarte

ALSO BY RACHEL ASTARTE

101 Better Sex Tips
The Bride of Manhattan
Celebrating Solitude

THE EXCHANGE

Rachel Astarte

Author photo: Chris Carroll

ISBN-10: 0615733050
ISBN-13: 978-0615733050

Printed in the United States of America.

This book is printed on acid-free paper.

For Patience, who inspired me to write this book.
For Khader, who continues to inspire me.

Contents

Too Hot to Trot   1

Damsel in 'Dis Dress   11

The Ol' Check-in Check-out   25

Funny Ha-ha   31

The Exchange   35

A Mod-ish Proposal   45

The Ice Cream Storm   51

The Stand-Up   55

Fox in Captivity   63

In the Line of Duty   69

Red Flags Flying   83

The Art of Love   93

The Adventures of David Astor   107

Getting Back on the ~~Hotel~~ Horse   115

There's No Place Like Phone   125

P.A. or P.I.?   129

Raising the Red Flag   137

The Biggest Game   143

The Wounded Warrior   147

A Family Affair   153

Handsome, Hair, and Hanuman   161

The Wounded Warrior Writes a Letter   173

Free Man in Paris   187

The Handsome Blues   207

Personal Assistance   215

Hooray for Bollywood   221

Operation Devdas   227

Oh, Brother, Where Art Thou?   235

sweet jesus, what have i done   241

You Can Go Home Again   263

Healing the Wounded Warrior   273

Busted   281

You Can Go Home Again (Take 2)   289

LA LA LA-LA   295

The Big O   303

The Little Mrs.   309

Jealous loving will make you crazy
if you can't find your goodness
'cause you lost your heart.
—Joni Mitchell

This was hardly an ideal evening for making love, meteorologically speaking. Ninety-eight degrees with no breeze. But tonight was Date Number Three with Jason Fanking, stand-up comedian and the first man to pay me any mind in two years. And hadn't my next-door-best-friend, Helen LoPresti burned into my pathetic little male-challenged brain that Date Number Three was the Magical Sex Date?

So. Jason and I ate Italian at Bricco's, since he swears by the scungilli there. (Personally, I found it a little too scungy, but never mind.) Afterwards, I watched Jason's scathingly witty set at the Catch A Rising Star comedy club, basking the self-important glow of being the date of the guy in the spotlight...until Jason used me for his act, observing that my blouse was so colorful it looked "like Jackson Pollock yacked on it."

But I'd come this far and was not to be deterred. At the end of our date, I ran the whole "I really have to get up early, but you're welcome to come up for a coffee" routine, and—joy of joys!—we ended up here in my bed for the inevitable. Just like in a film.

Helen would be so proud...once Jason was gone and I ran across the hall to tell her, that is. I rely heavily on Helen for dating guidance. She is an expert; I most definitely am not.

Not that I don't want to be. I love men. But attracting them been has always been a slight problem. Helen has no idea why. As she says, I'm "a hot little package of athletic flesh" (mostly because my job as a personal assistant keeps me running like a madwoman around the city). To be fair, I do have nice hair. Thick, straight, honey-brown. I have a face that has been described by the few men I've dated as "cute," and a bust size that the same men have politely not described at all. Yeah, so, the titty fairy ran out of dust by the time she got to my house. I've learned to live with it. What else can you do that doesn't cost seven grand?

The tragedy is this: Even if I could catch a man, I wouldn't have the first clue what to do with him. I mean, in the long run. What if I discover that he's an insensitive jerk, a liar, or—worse still—married? I work my mind into this whirlwind of anxiety, blaming men I haven't met yet for infractions they haven't had a chance to commit. But then I psyche myself into believing I'm worthy of the game. (*Others play it, why can't I?*) I put on a smile, buy a sixty-dollar push-up bra, and get back on the horse with the intent to gallop into the urban sunset. But you see, that's the moment when this other niggling question pops into my head: *What's the point?*

Why spend the first half of my adult life trying to find a partner to spend the other half with? If I never find him, won't I have wasted years that I could have spent developing my own happiness? If I hadn't bought into the fairy tale that someday my prince will come, I could have gone to Calcutta and worked with orphans. Learned Sanskrit and translated ancient texts that could have enlightened the world. I could have become a scientist and maybe found the cure for cancer/AIDS/Parkinson's/Alzheimer's/the common cold.

But like most women, I chose the easy way—to play this game of love—which is, as I quickly discovered, *not* easy at all. And now, at thirty-four, I still hadn't found a mate. While I enjoyed living alone, the thought of dying that way scared the stuffing out of me.

That's why Jason had to be The One; I didn't know how much more of this dating agony I could take. So, there I lay, my head banging out a rhythmic but not altogether unpleasant beat against my headboard. Something along the lines of a Sousa march. Despite the scorching weather, I didn't mind our patriotic lovemaking; the only male member that had visited my bed in the last two years was a slab of silicone named "Vlad The Impaler."

"Oh, Norah," Jason whispered playfully in my ear. "I'm sweating all over you. How rude."

"I don't mind. Really."

"It was a joke."

I grimaced.

Jason's body resumed its *slap-slap* against mine like a slab of beef tossed on a butcher counter. This was an image I pushed away in favor of concentrating on climaxing before I suffered heat stroke. I could already imagine the cold shower I'd take after Jason had gone. Oh, the cool droplets pelting my steaming skin...that was just enough bliss to send me right over the edge.

I moaned and Jason moved faster, making little grunting noises. I was sure he was right there with me, but as I began my skin-rippling wave of orgasm, Jason collapsed on top of me.

He was laughing.

"Oh, lord! That's perfect!" said Jason, and slid half way off me, groping across the top of the nightstand. "Do you have something I can write with?"

I cringed and grasped the edge of the mattress as the wave crashed and left me stranded in the ocean.

"Never mind." Jason hopped off me and zipped right out of the room on a pen-and-paper hunt as though he'd been doing nothing more than a few push-ups. "Can I write on this?" he called from the living room.

I sighed and folded my arms behind my head. *If I weren't so desperate,* I thought. *And if he weren't so cute. And funny. And hung. I'd dump him like a load of gravel.*

But why was I surprised? In the two-and-a-half weeks we'd been dating, it wasn't at all uncommon for Jason to tune out while I was talking and frantically scribble into the tattered notebook he always carried with him.

He didn't have his notebook tonight, though. Why would he? We were supposed to be making love. Our magical first time. The time we'd always remember. The time...

"This? Can I write on this?" Jason stood in the doorway of the bedroom, stark naked and semi-hard. I was fairly sure the woody was for his new joke, not me.

"That's Baz's travel itinerary. Use the pad by the phone."

Jason bounded off. Well, it was obvious: There would be no more nookie tonight. Jason was busy screwing his muse.

Now would have been the perfect time for a post-coitus-interruptus cigarette. That is, if I hadn't quit smoking six months ago. At the moment, I couldn't imagine why I'd ever done such a stupid thing.

I went into the living room and flipped on the television. Jason was already sitting on my couch, hunched over the coffee table, writing away with his tongue wedged in the corner of his lip. This is exactly what I was talking about. If only someone could have warned me that Jason was a joker in bed. Literally.

"I'm going to shower," I said. At least I'd have one corporeal pleasure tonight. I craned my neck to read what Jason had written on my telephone pad. I could only make out one word: *Sportfucking.*

Huh. Not bad.

I turned to head for the shower just as Jason blurted, "Hey, isn't that Baz?"

Sure enough, there was Baz on the TV screen in front of midtown Manhattan's Rihga Royal Hotel. Seeing Basil Vancouver on television was no big deal. He was the hunky British star of the prime time cop drama, *Handsome Blue,* and recently voted as one of the Top 10 Eligible Imports on *Access Hollywood.* He also happened to be my boss.

For the last six years, I'd had the distinct pleasure of being Baz Vancouver's personal assistant, his right hand, his gal Friday-through-Thursday. While he was working in New York, anyway. There was an L.A. assistant, but I'd never met her. I actually enjoyed not knowing anything about The Other Woman, as I playfully referred to her. It made me feel like some exotic courtesan in so many of the Bollywood films I often rented as a treat at the end of a long day. (As though there ever was an "end" to my day.)

You see, Baz's happiness and safety were not my responsibilities wherever else in the world he may have found himself. I needed only to concern myself with Baz's well-being while he was on my island territory, which was during the *Handsome Blue* shooting season. However, this never stopped him from frantically calling me in the middle of the night, as he did last summer from the *Fly By Night* film shoot (in which he played a clairvoyant stalker) asking me to ship him his Creatine supplements because The Other Woman had no idea where to find *his* brand. For some reason, whenever Baz mentioned TOW, I pictured a twiggy blonde with a vapid stare.

"Man, lookit all the cops. What'd he do?" Jason asked, giddy as a school kid. On television, lights flashed, paparazzi shoved their way in toward a quick-moving cluster of human bodies: two burly he-men, three cops, and little Basil Vancouver.

Now I registered that Baz was clad in nothing but his black silk pajama bottoms and reading glasses. His spiky blondette hair (the color he created to describe his brunette-with-bleached-blonde tufts) was deliciously unkempt. The whole package made him look like some dreamy Hollywood hybrid. Part James Dean, part Jude Law, but one hundred-percent Baz Vancouver. Cute as he was, he was now also in peril. And in my world, that just wasn't acceptable.

"Turn up the sound," I said, trancelike.

"As far as we can tell," said the stone-faced NY1 reporter, "no one has been hurt. The young man in question says he will not press charges."

"Oh, shit." Jason barely suppressed a laugh.

"Shh."

On the television screen, Baz lifted a small silver cell phone to his ear.

From the bedroom, my mobile tinkled, "I Can't Get No Satisfaction." I raced in and whipped the phone off the nightstand.

"Baz?"

"Petal," said Baz in a pouty voice. "I imagine you're watching this foolishness?"

I was back out in the living room in a flash. Baz looked directly into the camera, right at me. "For god's sake, Basil, what happened?"

Jason spun around on the couch. "Is that *him*?" I rolled my eyes.

"Nothing, I swear. I had a new little friend over and we, uh, tipped over a few tables...in the lobby—"

"Oh, no."

"—but that was only *after* he called me a sell-out snob just because I didn't feel like *fisting* him at that particular moment." Baz yelled this in the direction of someone off-screen.

"Lord." I braced myself against the wall, trying to not let my mind linger on images of animal husbandry. "What do they want you to do?"

"Oh, you know, sign a few things. Then I thought I might pop round for a nightcap. What say you?"

"Basil, did you get kicked out of the Rihga? The only home you've known in New York for the past six years? The arrangement that took me months to set up all nice-nice for you?"

"A tad."

"For how long?"

"Ever. I think."

I sighed. "I'll be right there."

"Oh, love! Do you have any of my Opaline body bath on hand?"

"Always."

I did not have any Opaline body bath in the house. It was just not in my nature to keep $200 bath goo lying around. But God knows I'd have some by the time he got here.

"I adore you." Baz clicked off. On the television screen, he made a little wink at the camera, ostensibly to alert his fans that all was A-OK, but I knew the wink was all mine.

"I have to go," I said.

Jason shrugged and clicked over to Comedy Central. "No problem."

I tossed Jason his shorts and T-shirt. "That means *you* have to go. But it's been a pleasure. I hope we can do it again real soon-like."

"Is that sarcasm I smell?"

"Tell the cabbie to take FDR Drive downtown," I yelled from the bedroom as I gave it a quick scan to be sure Jason hadn't left anything. "It's out of the way, but there's major overnight construction on Second Avenue."

"You're a wonder, Wonder Woman!"

The front door slammed shut.

I checked the clock; I had approximately fourteen minutes before Aquatique—the only shop where I could pick up Baz's Opaline—closed for the night.

Forget the fact that I smelled like a French whore on Bastille Day: I had to get in a cab, pick up the Opaline, fly over to the Rihga Royal, and somehow smooth things out with the authorities without doing irreparable damage to Baz's career as a television icon.

But first I'd need to put on some clothes.

The cab sped up and I got in, barely having a moment to decide the best route from my Yorkville apartment on 84th Street down to Midtown West. Before I knew it, Mr. Cab Guy was heading toward Second Avenue. I had grabbed the first thing I saw in my closet—a gauzy white wraparound dress—and the whole thing was already sticking to my sweat-soaked body.

"No, no!" I cried, tugging my dress out from between my legs. "Other way, damn it! FDR Drive!"

"You did not say this," said the apathetic cabbie. "Second Avenue quicker."

"*Not* quicker. Christ, have you been driving around this city at all in the last week? There's—" Before I had a chance to say the word, the cab came upon pylons, smoke stacks billowing from the cement, and a bunch of yellow-slickered men waving individual cars past at the rate of congealing pudding.

Time check: Ten minutes. I tossed a fiver up to the driver and ran out of the cab, hot-footing it through the sultry night. White gauze stuck to my thighs like bandages, but I kept it from creeping too far into indecency by whisking my hand over it every few steps.

I could see the awning of Aquatique. They seemed to still be open; the blue-green spotlight illuminated the gilded sign out front.

"Don't close, don't close, don't close...." I muttered my mantra with each quick-paced pad of my foot hitting the pavement. But just as I reached the door, it closed in front of me. And locked.

"No!" I banged my open palms on the door. "Please," I beseeched no one, "Fifteen seconds!"

The young male clerk sauntered over and pointed to the CLOSED sign. "I know what I need," I mouthed. *Yeah, a shower*, I thought.

He shrugged exaggeratedly as though I was asking him to alter the time-space continuum—something that was, sadly, not in his job description. I collected myself, withdrew a twenty from my purse and touched it to the glass door. The young man smiled.

But it wasn't at the cash. He seemed to be staring lower than that, in the general locality of my chest. I knew even before I looked down. I thought I'd felt a pleasant and inexplicable breeze...

Indeed, my left breast had freed itself, smothered as it must have been, from its wraparound gauze enshrinement. But, oh, that was not the worst of it. Just above my nipple was a deep red and very fresh hickey.

I yanked the dress closed again and stared the clerk boldly in his face. He unlocked the door. I bolted past him to the fourth aisle before he had a chance to comment.

Nimbly, I wiggled my fingers along the shelf of delicately packaged bath lotions, potions, douses, and spritzes. "Fuck me, where is Opaline?" I stepped back and craned my neck to see the tissue-papered prize there on the very top shelf, just out of my reach.

"Must be only supermodels and giraffes shop here." I mumbled as I grabbed a loofa from a nearby rack and wedged a toe between the row of bathbeads on the bottom shelf. As stealthily as possible, I hoisted myself up and poked at the boxes, hoping, somehow that I could make only one of them fall into my free open hand.

Suddenly a body came too close to me and reached far above my head, taking down one of the tissue-papered boxes I'd just managed to loosen from the display.

"All you had to do was ask," said the clerk, flashing a smarmy smile. I let the loofa go limp.

"Are you saying I'm short?"

He shrugged.

"Well, screw you, because I am perfectly self-sufficient, short or not."

The clerk gave me a queer look. The smarminess of his smile shifted to something more piteous. After all, what kind of woman runs around late at night with hickeyed tit, a desperate need for Opaline, and still has the gall to stand her moral ground?

"I'll ring you out over here," he said. Then he walked away. I had no time to feel indignant; I had to get to Baz, and fast.

Eleven city blocks and four avenues later, I arrived at the Rihga Royal, out of breath from running, clutching tight to the frilly little box of Baz's bath goo.

The cops were still there, milling about, writing in pads of paper, mumbling into walkie-talkies, but no one seemed too upset except the hotel manager, who kept running his fingers through his thinning hair. As I approached Baz, the paparazzi turned on me full force, snapping photos like mad. I've often thought that paparazzi were much like the mafia: Shoot first, ask questions later. But I was used to the crowding in, the clattering of video equipment. I even recognized a few of the regulars. After all these years, I didn't even bother to cover my face anymore.

"Forget it, guys," shouted one of photographers. "It's just the assistant."

I made my way through the photohogs who were now seeking out Baz's young boy toy. Some of them greeted me as they passed; we'd been through five seasons together, after all.

"How's it hangin', Norah?"

"Hi, Larry. Hey, Rob."

Baz sat sulking in a corner of the lobby, nursing an Evian. I strode up to him, clearly miffed. "I got your Ovaltine, Grandma."

"Cheers, Petal. Can we go home now?"

"Not quite." I scanned the crowd and my gaze rested on a muscular young man who was giving his account of the evening to a couple of reporters. I gave a bullish huff through my nose and headed in his direction.

"I think you're done here," I told the reporters, never taking my eyes off the boy. The reporters dropped back, but lingered, probably hoping for more fireworks. "I think you're done here, too," I told the boy toy. "You got to Baz, and now your little game is over."

"All I wanted was an autograph," the kid whimpered at the reporters. "And he wouldn't give it to me."

"Yeah?" I turned my back on the cameras and whispered low in the boy's ear. "And how was Mr. Vancouver supposed to give you an autograph with his hand shoved up your ass?"

I turned to leave, but the kid gripped my arm. Hard. "Hey, fag hag."

Suddenly, all I could register was the blinding flash of instinctive animal fury. My face twitched and I tensed myself, prepared to haul off and deck him.

"I can still press charges, you know," he hissed at me.

I took one look at his hand on my arm, then back up at him. "So can I," I said through clenched teeth.

"I've got it all right here, Norah," said Larry, lifting his video camera.

15

I winked at the poor dumb kid. Or maybe it was another facial twitch. Didn't matter. "Why don't you just run along home now and forget this ever happened?"

"Doubtful," said the boy.

As soon as he got in the door of my apartment, Baz headed straight to my liquor cabinet.

"Just give me a minute to find you another hotel," I told him as he poured us both Bourbons.

"It's two in the a.m., Norah. I'll just crash on the couch," he handed me the drink. "If you don't mind."

"Baz, that's not appropriate."

"I'll behave."

"What I mean, you big hunk of throbbing libido, is that tomorrow you will have to walk down my five flights of stairs and out my front door, and onto the street, where the press will be waiting like a pack of starving wolves."

I crooked my finger at Baz and he followed me to the window. Downstairs, a few photohogs were milling around, looking upward, trying to guess which apartment was mine.

"Seeing you trouncing out of your assistant's apartment the morning after I nearly beat the living breath out of your studly suitor is not the kind of story we want developing before your new season begins."

Baz raised his eyebrows. "Isn't it? You know as well as I do, love: All press is good press."

"If I were a glamorous and high-priced call girl, maybe. But this won't do. Personal assistants *do not exist*. We skulk around in the shadows, living only for our celebrities. We're like special little fairies."

"Oo, speaking of special little fairies, didn't you think my Gio was lovely?"

"Was that his name? I didn't catch it." I quickly jotted it on my telephone pad.

"Granted, he was completely prickish," Baz continued fervently, "but he was *gorgeous*."

"Basil. Pay attention to me. Here's what's going to happen: You'll draw a nice hot bath, and you'll get in it with your drink and new little sudsies. By the time you towel off, I'll have found you a new place to live. There has to be some way to slip you out the back before the press figures out where 'the back' is. And then all will be well. 'Kay?" I plastered on my Mary Poppins smile.

Of course it would be. I never failed to make everything right. Under my care, Baz had never wanted for anything. There was no mess I couldn't pull him out of. Most of the time, I was expert at avoiding altercations before they even occurred. Like the season before he came out of the closet and I rerouted our limo around the Gay Pride Parade just so there would be no public confusion.

17

"Give a shout if you need anything," I yelled when the bathroom door had shut. And once I heard the bath water running, I cracked open my Little Black New York Resource Book.

Over my years of personal assistanthood, I had created lists of everything Baz would ever need—from gyms to jam shops. Oh, I know it's old school to have an actual book, not a nifty little series of spreadsheets available to me with the click of an app, but I love touching actual pages. Printing out information, slipping the paper into plastic sheaths, hearing that satisfying *click* as I snap them into the binder. Besides, when the grid finally crashes and the Internet implodes, I'll be prepared.

I leafed through the Living Space section of the book—demarcated with a stately blue divider—and called all the hotels I could find. But it was the same story with each one:

"I'm looking for a room for Mr. Baz Vancou—"

"Tonight? Uh, I—I don't think we have a, uh—" they'd stutter.

It seemed everyone had seen the news. Either that or they were just plain booked up. I ran through my entire list and then flipped open my laptop and did a frantic search for hotels in the area. After ten minutes and the realization that I'd already tried most of them, I burst into tears.

Actually, it was only one or two tears. The first vocal explosion of what would have been a sob was instantly cut off by that burly part of my brain, my internal drill sergeant, that demanded: *Cut the crap. You have work to do.*

Through a teary blur, I looked down at the computer screen. Hotel Ursula. I must have missed that one. In fact, I'd never even heard of it.

I said a quick prayer under my breath as I dialed.

"Hotel Ursula," said a soft female voice at the other end of the line. I'd probably woken her up.

I cleared my throat and put on my best professional voice. "Yes, hello. I realize that this is a late call, but I'm in urgent need of a room for Mr.—" I stopped short. "Mr. Charles—uh," I stared up at the ceiling to think. "Skye. Mr. Charles Skye. Do you have an availability?"

"One moment."

One moment felt like a week. Greek music played in the background. I was just getting into the whole Zorba vibe when she clicked back on.

"I'm sorry, all we have available is the Presidential Suite."

I could have crawled through the phone and kissed her for the fact that the Hotel Ursula was even in possession of a Presidential Suite.

"Perfect. But I have to ask that when we arrive—we'll be there in an hour or so—that Mr. Skye is not disturbed at all. I mean, I need the absolute minimum of people around. He's—uh—got a condition." Oh. I'm a genius. "It's a very serious condition, which is why we have to check in at night. He is severely agoraphobic, you see, and so it's imperative that—"

"Reservation for Skye. See you in an hour."

She clicked off.

Well, fine. One big hairy problem solved, one to go: How to get Baz out of my building without a fuss and not have him followed. There was the back fire escape. But there was only one way I could get to it.

"Baz?" I yelled. "I found you a place."

Baz stuck his head out of the bathroom. A whooff of steam billowed out. "Petal, you're a star."

"I'll be right back. Get dressed."

I scooted down the hall to Helen's apartment and rang the bell. She arrived at the door, quick-wrapped in a pink chenille bathrobe, her head a symphony of tousled amber curls. "Norah. Is everything all right? Are you on fire?"

"Not really. I mean, I'm not on fire. I have Baz."

"It that a rash type of thing?" she asked, rubbing her eyes.

"Baz," I said again, pointedly. "Basil Vancouver. He's in my apartment."

Helen's eyes widened and she looked past my shoulder down the hall to my half-open door. "He's here? In this actual building?"

I nodded. She regarded my sweat-stained slip of a dress and her eyes bugged even more.

"He went *straight*? Oh, but this is magical!"

"No, no. It's a long story. There's press outside and I need to get him out of here. I thought I could slip him down your fire escape."

"Let me get this right. You want to sneak the hunkiest and most talented actor in Hollywood into my apartment and down my rusty old fire escape into Crack Alley?"

"I don't know what else to do, Hel," I whined. "My brain isn't functioning anymore."

Helen tightened her robe. "Give me five minutes. I'll be right over."

Baz was already toweled off, moisturized, and neatly dressed in black, tight-fitting pants and a silk T when I got back.

"What's the plan, then?" He asked perkily, as though we were in some role-playing adventure game.

"We're slipping you out the back."

"Who's 'we'?"

Perfectly on cue, Helen waltzed into my apartment, wearing perhaps the hottest—and tiniest—dress I have ever seen. It was a haute red number. The neckline and hemline longed so deeply for each other that they seemed to be struggling to meet halfway. Her hair was loose and flowing, eyes smoky and lips blood red. She'd even powdered her cleavage so that it shone nearly incandescent.

Baz sat frozen on the couch in stunned silence for a moment, and then lifted his fingertips to his slightly open mouth.

"This is 'we'," I told him. "And," I turned to Helen, "what is it that 'we' have in mind?"

"First thing's first," said Helen, gliding over to Baz. She took his hand and bent toward him, offering a view of her delectables. "Helen LoPresti. It is an honor to finally meet you, Mr. Vancouver. I'd say I'm your biggest fan, but I'm not a competitive person—"

"Helen! We don't have time for this."

"*Tss*," Baz hissed at me, never taking his eyes off Helen.

"I have watched *Handsome Blue* since the very first episode when your Officer Smithy was just the goofy little rookie—"

"Goofy? I don't think—"

"—and I have not missed one show since. Ask Norah."

"I will do," said Baz with a smirk.

"Congrats on making Captain last season."

"Cheers."

"Now, I know you're gay and all, but I have a very sexy little plan in mind."

"Yes, well... Helen, is it?" said Baz, clearing his throat. "Since you bring it up, I'd have to say my sexuality is most accurately likened to a tropical garden. Have a seat here next to me and I'll explain—"

"No. Time. Baz," I said, pounding the wall with my fist.

"Here's my plan," Helen said, hoisting up each of her breasts, one at a time, and letting them fall back down into the dress for maximum buxosity. "Mr. Vancouver and I are going to leave out the front door."

"What?" I screeched.

"Together. Arm in arm. It'll confuse the crap out of them."

"Forget it, Helen. You'll both end up on the cover of every rag in the country."

Helen smiled naughtily. "Oh? How awful."

Baz straightened. "My god, she's right. It's the perfect antidote to tonight's travesty with that little Gio prick. They won't know what to think of me!"

"Except that you're a big slut," I huffed.

Both Helen and Baz shot me the same look. Point taken.

I trailed The Happy Couple, calling for the car as Baz and Helen breezed out of my building with their arms intertwined. Helen even stole a few kisses on Baz's neck.

As the photohogs snapped their libelous pictures, a few reporters called out things like, "Busy night, Baz!" and "Hey, Baz, changing camps?" But Basil took it all in stride. I opened the car door for the royal couple and got into the front with the driver.

The whole ordeal was over in forty-five seconds.

The Ol' Check-in Check-out

How many times had I walked along the Fifth Avenue side of Central Park and assumed the Hotel Ursula was just another huge brownstone apartment building? When the car dropped us off, there was not a soul on the street. Not so much as a filthy rich insomniac walking his dog.

I sent the car back, with Helen in it, after Baz expressed his undying gratitude by kissing her full on the lips. I knew quite well that I'd be hearing about that pinnacle moment in Helen's life for the rest of my own. A small price to pay. She had bailed us out, after all.

"Baz," I said, once we'd gotten inside, "Why don't you have a seat here at the bar until I get you checked in? And put your sunglasses on."

"Really, Norah. There's no one here."

My lip quivered in frustration. Baz shrugged, slipped his Prada shades on, and parked himself on a stool.

There was no one at the registration desk. I gave half a thought to ringing the bell that was sitting there, but this place was so quiet that I thought it would be in terrible taste to ruin the peace. I picked up a pen and flicked the bell.

Pingk.

Nothing.

Pingk-pingk.

Oh, man.

Pingly-ping-ping-ping.

"Yes?" A young, crisply dressed woman appeared from the back room.

"I'm sorry. I'm here to check in Ba—I mean, Mr. Charles Skye."

She sighed. "Presidential Suite."

"Yes. That's it."

"Where is Mr. Skye?"

"Over there. At the bar."

"The bar is closed."

"He knows that. I told you. He has a condition. No human conta—"

"I'll need to see his identification."

"I'm sorry?"

"Driver's license, passport?"

"What for?"

"Hotel policy."

"But I'll be paying for the suite."

"I understand. It's for security purposes." She gave me a very weary look. "Yours and ours."

This couldn't be happening. Not now. Not at three in the blessed morning. Not after all I'd been through tonight. I was not going to let one more little person with his or her little quirky demands stop me from doing my job.

On another occasion, say a bright spring afternoon or perhaps after I'd had a decent shower and didn't feel like I'd been sweat-wrestling frat boys, I might have complimented her taste in frocks or appealed to our common denominator of working for The Man, but now? Now I was cranky, stinky, sexually unsatisfied, and entirely fed up.

I leaned in and laid on my best Hannibal Lecter *sotto voce*. "Listen to me very carefully. See that man over there? He is not Mr. Charles Skye. He is Mr. Basil Vancouver. Two-time Emmy-winner and film star. Now, I'm sure that you, along with millions of others, have seen the news tonight, but I'm even more sure that I don't give two shits. Mr. Vancouver needs this room, and he will have it now. He will show no identification. And that is for *his* security, and his alone." I slammed my purse on the counter.

"I am his assistant, Norah Pasquale. I am now going to take this American Express card," I held it up and ran my finger along the bottom, "that clearly bears *my name* and pay for his room—which he will need indefinitely—in advance of one week. Then you are going to give me the key to the Presidential Suite and I am going to make sure Mr. Vancouver gets tucked in all safe and cozy with no incidents. Once that has been accomplished, I am going to go home, get into bed, and slip gently into a coma."

The woman blinked twice, then picked up the receiver of a big red phone on the wall behind her.

"Oh, no. What are you doing?" I moaned. "Don't use The Big Red Phone. Who is that?"

She turned away from me, spoke quickly and quietly, and then hung up. "One minute, please. You can wait with your movie star friend, if you'd like."

I looked over my shoulder, toward the bar. Baz was sitting in the darkened room with his sunglasses still on, engrossed in some kind of bar napkin origami project.

Just then, one of the elevators made its slow descent to the lobby. The door clacked open, and an ornate gate was pulled aside. As if in deliriously slow motion, out stepped a tall, painfully beautiful man. He wore all-white, gauzy linen pajamas, the perfect fabric match to my own dress, although his outfit was much the better for wear.

The shirt was open to mid-chest, exposing a healthy expanse of dark hair, the same color as the longish waves on his head. His drawstring trousers were rolled up to the ankles. His feet were bare. For a moment I thought the desk clerk had a hotline to the heavens and had called down Adonis to punish me.

As the Man in White passed the bar, Baz dropped his napkin swan and moved to get off his barstool. I pointed in a firm downward fashion and he sat back down. As the man came closer, I could see his olive skin was slightly rumpled with sleep, his dark eyes bleary. He glided by me and gave a look that I was sure was sheer hatred but could just as easily have been one of single-minded purpose.

That was when I smelled him. A warm, musk-spicy, fresh-out-of-bed, unequivocally male scent. I grabbed the reception counter with both hands in order to remain upright.

The woman whispered something to him as he stepped around the counter and punched a few keys on a computer. He chewed a little on his lower lip as he regarded the information on the screen, leaving the lip glistening. The gesture nearly rendered me unconscious.

The Man in White reached around behind him to the wall of hotel keys and removed a shiny brass one. Holding it above my hand, he turned his eyes on me. They were the color of bittersweet chocolate, and I wanted nothing more than to suck them right out of his head.

The key dropped into my open palm. I parted my lips to thank him but no sound came out.

Without a word, the Man in White padded back around the counter, past the slack-jawed movie star at the bar, and into the elevator, which clacked shut and re-ascended to the heavens.

I collected myself and closed my fingers around the key. "I'm sorry," I said to the woman. "I didn't mean for you to call your manager."

"I didn't," she said curtly. "That was the owner."

Funny Ha-ha

"I'm not telling you what to do," Helen flicked the butt of her Capri Menthol into the gutter as we headed back into Funny Ha-Ha, the hot new East Village comedy club.

I'd like to say we got our VIP seats about a foot from the stage solely because I was the headliner's girlfriend—billing me thusly to the door person was obviously Jason's way of saying I'm sorry for the sex we barely had. But our optimum seating could have also been due to the fact that Helen's face was plastered all over the inside of several tabloids that week, catapulting her to semi-celebrity status.

"I just think that if you put a little more effort into it, you could snag Jason in a big way. He's obviously attracted." Helen gesticulated with the hand still holding her pack of smokes, making me want a cigarette even more.

"Until he's *dis*-tracted," I mumbled into my whiskey sour.

"Don't let him get distracted. That's exactly my point! You need to do the dance, Norah."

"I hate the dance."

"I know, but we are animals. There is a dance that all of nature's creatures have to do in order to keep a mate. You want that, don't you?"

"To be Mrs. Funny Ha-ha? I don't know."

Helen squeezed the last drops of juice from the lime wedge in her vodka tonic. "Okay, then try this: Imagine him with a sitcom."

"His own show, or a featured character on someone else's show?"

"Christ, Norah. Don't be difficult. It's 'The Jason—' What's his last name again?" I pointed to the poster on the wall. "Fanking? 'The Jason *Fanking* Show'? That's terrible."

"Sure is unfortunate."

"God! You'll be Norah Fanking!"

"I most certainly will not."

"Not at this rate, you won't. Look at you moping over here with me when you should be humping him in the boiler room."

"Helen, the man interrupted our very first lovemaking session to write down a joke. I'm not the one who needs to make an effort."

"So? He's devoted to his art."

"Please. Maybe he's just not The One. I just wish I knew that before I bothered going to bed with him." I swigged down the rest of my drink. "That's how it always is. I invest time and emotion in a man only to find out a few weeks or even months down the line that he's an egomaniac or a closet racist or an ex-con—"

"God, where have you been picking up men?"

"I'm serious, Helen. We women do research before we buy a damned handbag. Doesn't it make sense to get some background on the man we could be spending the rest of our life with?"

Helen cocked her head and gave me a squinty, considering look.

"What?"

She grabbed my hand and squeezed it. "I will answer that question, but not right now. Right now you need to go find Jason and give him a good luck grope."

"I can't go backstage."

Helen wilted. "Of course you can. You're VIP, dummy."

I sighed. She was right. "Give me a cigarette first," I said, eyeing her pack.

"No way."

"Don't be a hero, Helen. I'm nervous as all hell and I need one of your little girlie smokes, there."

"Stop stalling," said Helen. She shoved my chair backwards with her stilettoed foot.

Back stage was really only a few feet away, so Helen got the full view of what happened next. For Helen's benefit I burlesqued a tip-toe across to the other side of the stage, where a production assistant told me he last saw Jason. I stopped at the heavy red velvet curtain and made a big show of throwing it aside.

There, leaning against the fake brick wall set was Jason, ramming his tongue down the throat of a semi-shirted womanchild wearing a headset and carrying a clipboard. Her right leg was hiked up around Jason's waist, arms a tangle around his neck. One of his hands was flat against the brick and the other was in between their bodies, somewhere out of sight. I could only guess.

When I regained the use of my brain, it registered that there were several people laughing behind me. Helen was howling. Oh, not in laughter. It was more like a primal, mama-lion death roar.

"You raging asshole!" I think was how it manifested itself in English.

Before I knew it, Helen had my elbow and I was being yanked away from the spectacle just in time for Jason to disengage his lips from the techie-chick and try to use them to say something to me. But I never heard him. In the last second before the front door closed behind us, I lifted my right hand and flipped Jason the bird.

I fought every urge in my body not to say to Helen what was truly on my mind on the cab ride home. But the words rang in my ears, nonetheless: *I told you so. All men are shit. I will now take a vow of celibacy and wed myself to my work.* As though the latter would be any different from my life as it already was.

Even as we got to my apartment and Helen made me a stiff cup of Indian chai, I said nothing. I just sat curled up on my couch, contemplating which leading man in which of my Bollywood rentals would rejuvenate my belief in true love. There was a science to this decision: If the hero was cute, fine. Eye candy. I'd feel better. But if he was too cute, it inevitably got me thinking about my own prospects for Perfect Love, and that got me depressed.

"I bet The Man in White would never cheat," I told the stack of DVDs I was fanning out on the coffee table.

"Who's The Man in White?" asked Helen, taking one of the boxes. "One of your little Indian crushes?"

"Never mind," I said, deflated.

"I have something that'll make you feel better." Helen put her tea mug on the coffee table with a pronounced thud. She flipped open my laptop and opened the web browser. "I promise it'll fix your man problems."

"Cyberporn doesn't cut it for me."

"Here," she plopped the computer in my lap. "Type in 'theexchange.com'."

I did what she said and the screen turned pink. Cutsie little animated icons of shoes, bags, necklaces, trousers, blouses, and the like started dancing around the edges of the screen. In the background, the New York City skyline sparkled like diamonds.

"What is this?"

"Just what it says," said Helen, pointing to the banner at the top. It read: THE EXCHANGE. "You enter what you're looking for—eveningwear, business suit, whatever—and then the size, type, color and date you need it. Then you get a list of items that other women have and are willing to lend you. In turn, you enter information on whatever you might have in *your* closet."

"This is how you answer my question about the dangers of dating men we know nothing about? I should trade my wardrobe with other single women in New York in the hopes of trapping one anyway?"

Helen bit her lip. "No."

"You're being weird. What's going on?"

She took my *TV Guide* and wrote two words at the bottom of the Tylenol ad on the back:

ROOKIE

innersanctum

"Log in with these. They're a temporary username and password for basic access."

"'Basic access'? What am I doing, exchanging trousers with Agent Scully?"

"Close enough."

Grimacing, I logged in. But just as I hit the Enter key, Helen put her hands over the screen. "Norah, what you are about to see is absolutely top-top supremo secret. You may not discuss it with anyone, not even me, outside of our own homes. Do you understand?"

"Well, if it's top-top *supremo* secret."

"I'm not joking. This is serious business."

"Wow. Okay. Sorry."

"All right." Helen took a grounding breath. "The thing you mentioned tonight at the club. About there being some way to find out about men before you get serious with them?"

"Yeah?"

"That thing exists."

Helen removed her hands from the screen. The dancing accessories had disappeared. The horrible girlie pink background was now black. From the top of the Empire State Building in the skyline, a string of red hearts continuously shot out and floated up to the top banner, wedging themselves between the "X" and the "C". The banner now read: THE EX♥CHANGE.

"What happened? What is this?"

"It's an underground database of single men in New York City, compiled by the thousands of women who have dated them."

"You've got to be kidding."

Helen shook her head. "Once you're a member, you can look up any man and read what other women have said about him. And if he's not in the database, you can add him yourself."

"How did I not know about this?"

"It's not as if you've been out there lately. But now you are, so—"

I stared at the screen. "This is surreal."

"I know! It was created by *one* woman, if you can believe that. Apparently, she's this brilliant entrepreneur who fell in love, got jilted, and was so hurt that she created the network to prevent any other woman from going through what she did."

"How magnanimous," I said, and clicked off the screen.

"Don't you want to give it a test run?"

"Oh, please. What I said at the club was just a fantasy, that's all. We're supposed to try and fail until we find the right person. It's part of 'the game', right?" Helen looked horrified. "Don't worry, Hel,

I won't tell anyone what I saw." I put up three fingers. "Galpal's honor."

"Do me a favor," Helen stood up. "Don't come crying to me when you get your heart broken by some egomaniacal racist ex-con, okay?"

"Why not?" I sipped my chai. "That's what best friends are for."

"Fine. Be that way." Helen grabbed her purse off the floor and jabbed it in the direction of my stack of DVDs. "Enjoy your evening all alone with Genghis Khan."

"*Aamir* Kha—forget it. Listen, Helen, maybe this sort of thing works for you," I waved my hand at the lifeless computer in my lap, "but it's just too high tech for me. I'm romantically challenged, remember?"

Helen softened and bent down to put her arms around me. "I'm sorry. You've had a rough night." She released me. "Take some time, think it over. If you decide to apply, you don't even have to let me know."

"Helen—"

"Norah? You know what you really need?"

"A swift bullet in my cortex?"

"A good whack-off."

"Oh, my."

"Definitely! You deserve it. Make yourself a little lavender oil bath, pour some bubbly, and just go at yourself. Believe me, it'll do you good."

"Great. G'night, Dr. LoPresti."

What had the world come to? A database for dishing dirt on men. Amazing. I laughed into my tea mug. Huh. I wonder how much time I would have saved, though, if I'd been able to look up some of these losers I'd been with over the years.

I tossed my laptop aside and popped into the DVD player one of my old standbys, *Zindagi Khoobsurat Hai*. Life is Beautiful. It was the love story of a wayward woman, a famous Hindi singer, and a mute kid. A real love-stained tear-jerker. Just what I needed.

God only knows what drew me to Bollywood. Maybe it was the belief that love is holy. Like the Hindu story of Krishna and Radha. They were married to other people, but their devotion to each other was so strong and pure that even today they're worshipped as a couple: The symbol of true love.

Or maybe it was just the singing and dancing. No matter what was going on in the film—a biker bar fight with broken bottles or the moment a spoiled rich girl realizes she's fallen for her innocently puckish chauffeur—the whole town burst into song and eventually some happy couple would end up spinning, open-armed on a mountain top in the Swiss Alps. And corny as the whole thing may seem, it gave me great hope to see straight men who knew how to move their hips when they danced.

But halfway through *Zindagi...*, I kept thinking about The Exchange. This whole pulsating underground organization that I was not a part of. Why wasn't I? I reopened my lap top and logged back on to The Exchange. I clicked the APPLY NOW button and a form screen popped up where I was asked to create a username and password. I thought for a moment, then typed in: BOLLYWOMAN. For my password, I typed in the second thing on my mind: HOTELURSULA.

Then there were a series of demographic questions: Age range, Marital status, Salary, Neighborhood, etc. There was even an initiation section where I had to give up the goods on one recent date. Of course, I entered Jason and clicked off a slew of unflattering traits from the pulldown menu: Cheater, Rude, Self-absorbed. But then I also selected Well-endowed. Credit where it was due, after all.

I clicked SUBMIT. A pop-up window thanked me and told me I'd be receiving a response in the next twenty-four hours.

Well, grand.

Still not ready to return to my colorful fantasy world of singing South Asian prostitutes and the men who loved them, I decided to do some research on Hotel Ursula. I had to update my New York Resource Book with vital stats on the place Baz was staying.

Yeah, right.

I found the Hotel Ursula website and clicked on the link to its background.

> Established in 1965, **Hotel Ursula** is an enchanting European-style hotel located in the heart of New York City. Owner and proprietor **Nikos Santos** offers his guests ultimate comfort with complimentary baskets of locally-grown fruit, optional breakfast-en-suite, turn down service, and morning *New York Times*. If you're in town for business, the **Millennium Conference Center** located in Times Square and owned by **Alexis Santos** is the perfect location for meetings or conferences. Business or pleasure, you can be assured friendly and professional service at this or any of the hotels owned and run by The Santos family group.

Nikos Santos. So that was the Man in White. I scrolled down to the bottom of the page. There were three more links:

<u>Francisco Santos</u>
> Hotel Yosefina (Taormina, Italy)
> Hotel Thalia (Athens, Greece)

<u>Nikos Santos</u>
> Hotel Ursula (New York City, USA)

<u>Alexis Santos</u>
> Millennium Conference Center (New York City, USA)

I sucked in a breath and clicked on his name. The screen went blank for a second and then a photo began to download. There was a little balloon with text above the picture:

Quick Facts: NIKOS SANTOS

Born:	February 19, 1967 (Taormina, Sicily)
Family:	Ursula (Mother, deceased) Francisco (Father) Alexis (Brother)
Holiday Spots:	Paris; Florence; Kazan
Favorite Food:	Green Tea Ice Cream

Green tea ice cream. Fascinating.

I scrolled down to the picture. A New York City rooftop, ostensibly of the Hotel Ursula. There, leaning against a railing, was Mr. Nikos Santos. He held a glass of red wine in one hand, his torso bent slightly forward, caught in mid-laugh. From the corners of his eyes fanned gentle lines. His lips were full, glistening, just as they were the night I first saw him.

I felt sick. No, really ill. Like I was going to throw up all over my computer. I slapped the lid of the laptop shut, raced to the bathroom, and flipped up the lid of the toilet. But nothing came. I just knelt there, taking deep breaths and meditating into the calm blue water within.

"What *was* that?" I asked no one. My body was on fire. My hands twitched. I rolled backwards and leaned against the tub. What a mess. A thought came to me, then: *You're not sick, idiot. You're turned on.* Imagine that. Maybe Helen's earlier suggestion wasn't such a bad one.

Slowly, I slid my hand down into my trousers and let a few fingers wander slowly. I pictured myself on the roof of The Hotel Ursula.

I have just finished telling hotel mogul Nikos Santos a deliciously wicked anecdote. He laughs—at which point a picture is snapped—and pulls me to him. Nikos Santos spirits me away to a quiet spot, where he...recognizes me as the bitch who ruined his sleep and caused his hotel clerk to quit her job, leaving him to run the entire place by himself until he could hire the type of help that guests of the Hotel Ursula have come to expect, which isn't easy to come by in this city...

Shit. It was a wonder I could sleep at night. Something was going to have to be done.

There was no choice: I would have to launch Operation Green Tea Ice Cream.

A Mod-ish Proposal

At nine-fifteen the next morning, Baz was scheduled to shoot a mob thug to death on 72nd Street and Columbus. According to my research, there were only two places on my route to the shoot where I could pick up green tea ice cream. The first, a gourmet health food shop on 64th and Broadway, was sold out. That left a small Japanese Shabu Shabu restaurant just across the street from the 72nd Street subway station. It took some convincing and an extra ten-spot, but I got the shy, somewhat-English-speaking hostess to sell me a pint.

Once I'd scored, I went straight to Baz's trailer on Amsterdam Avenue and slipped the treasure into his freezer for safekeeping until my planned delivery later that evening.

"Petal, you're not going to believe it," said Baz, hastily entering the trailer. He clicked the door shut and locked it. "It's happened."

He was in full wardrobe and makeup, but his shoulder holster was empty. That's when I noticed he had the gun in his hand.

"You finally shot the crafts caterer for not providing Branston Pickle."

Baz looked at the gun in his hand and immediately holstered it. "We just finished a take. I was so excited, I... Anyway, guess what?"

"I'm all a'titter. What is it?"

"Smithy's coming out! They wrote it into this season's storyline. Finally, after all my campaigning." He collapsed victoriously on the couch and ran his fingers through his well-slicked hair.

"Careful, Gina will never forgive me for letting you mess up the coif."

"Oh, right." He wiped his hands on his trousers. I winced. Now Harriet in wardrobe would hate me. "But isn't it fantastic?"

"Sure."

"That's not the best part. His love interest is going to be a brand new character. A Lieutenant in our Organized Crime and Vice Department played by—wait for it—none other than David Astor."

"David Astor. Wow. Is he nice?"

"You met him. On the film shoot last summer, *Fly By Night*? He played the husband of the woman I stalked. He hunted me down and we had that big tussle in the canyon?"

"Everyone knows who David Astor is, Baz, I'm saying I never met him. Must've been your Other Woman."

"Oh, right. Well, never mind. He's brilliant. You'll absolutely love him."

I cleared my throat. "So, how's the hotel? I mean, is it up to par and all? Are they treating you well?"

"Fabulous. Complete privacy. No one even looks at me twice. Kind of sad, really."

I leapt up. "Do you want me to find you somewhere else to stay? Because I can. It's no problem at all."

"Did I say that? My, but we're a bit panicky today, aren't we?" Baz regarded me for a moment. "What was that you were doing in my fridge?"

"What? Nothing. When?"

"Just now, when I came in. I haven't seen a door slam shut that fast since my mum caught me in her suspendies and bra." Baz opened the little fridge door. Except for a bottle of Zinfandel, it was empty. He looked at me.

"Freezer," I sighed.

He opened it and removed the pint. "Green tea ice cream? *Pour moi? Merci, mon petit chou.*"

"Actually, it's—"

Right. What was I planning to say? *It's a peace offering to that great big hunk of a hotel owner under whose roof you are so undeservedly privileged to sleep.*

"It's for later. You have to get ready for the Gray's Papaya shoot now."

Baz took the top off the ice cream and scooped some up with his finger, grinning like a mischievous child. "It's tomorrow. They rescheduled it this morning. You should know that, Norah." He sucked the ice cream off his finger. "You're slipping."

My face went hot. I could barely swallow. Baz tilted the pint in my direction. I shook my head. He shrugged and put it back in the freezer. There was no giving it to Mr. Nikos Santos now.

"Sorry, Baz. I was sure I had the latest schedule."

Baz removed his holster and began to unbutton his shirt with calculated rumination. "You know, Norah, I was going to ask you to come back to Los Angeles with me after this season is over. To be my assistant year-round—"

"You *what*?"

"—but now I just don't know. I'm not sure I can rely on you anymore."

I took his shirt from him and hung it up on the wardrobe rack. "Basil, really. This is our sixth season together. When have I ever let you down?"

"Today." He unbuckled his belt, slipped off his trousers and handed them to me. "Are you in love or something?"

"I'm just...I have a lot on my mind," I explained, turning my back. "That's no excuse, I know. I'm not supposed to have a life. And, as it turns out, I don't, but I...well, I'll be better. Sorry."

Baz began to laugh. I kept my back to him; there was no telling what state of undress he was in. "Why are you laughing?"

"You're incredible."

"Thank you?"

"They didn't reschedule the shoot, Norah. I was just taking the piss. It was a test of your loyalty."

I spun around. Baz was in nothing but boxers, and down on bended knee. He took my hand tenderly. "Norah Pasquale, will you—"

"This isn't happening."

"Shush. Norah Pasquale, will you be my full-time assistant? To tolerate, put up with, and otherwise platonically service—both here and in Los Angeles—until Hollywood does us part?"

"I...god, Baz—" I dropped his hand.

How could I leave New York? No reason to. Everything I needed was right here. It was my home. Not to mention that I certainly had no desire to go to L.A. and live *there* for half my life. But would Baz cut me loose for good if I said no? He was quite literally the reason I got out of bed in the morning. What would I do without his needing me?

Baz looked up at me sweetly, expectantly.

"Can I have some time to think about it?"

I realized then that I was still holding onto Baz's trousers. No, I was wringing them with both fists. That was when Harriet the wardrobe director came in. She took one look at the mangled trousers in my hands, Basil on one knee, made a throaty sound, and backed out of the trailer.

Baz got up and brushed himself off. "We'll be reading about this tomorrow. That woman has the biggest mouth."

"Sorry."

"Norah, love. You have got to stop apologizing. You're worse than a Brit." He opened the freezer and took out the ice cream again.

"Were you serious about the L.A. thing?"

"Deathly."

"You'll give me some time?"

"'Course. The season's just begun. Now shouldn't you be chastising me for lounging around in my knickers eating ice cream when I should be getting dressed for the Gray's Papaya shoot?"

"That means I have to get Harriet back in here with your clothes, doesn't it."

Baz nodded, ruefully. "I'd hate to have your job."

I stepped cautiously into the lobby of the Hotel Ursula, half expecting the Crazy-Lady-In-Need-Of-Anger-Management alarms to go off. But all was perfectly peaceful. A quiet bustle of comings and goings. Some guests lounged in the lobby drinking pints from the bar and perusing travel maps of NYC. An older French couple was just checking in as I approached the registration desk.

It hadn't been as much trouble as I thought it might be scoring another pint of green tea iced cream from the Shabu Shabu place after I left Baz's trailer. This time around, however, the hostess wasn't too shy to bring over the entire wait staff to bow their thanks for my excessive albeit odd patronage.

For some reason, the gods were smiling on me in another way: The front desk clerk was not the same woman I'd encountered when I checked Baz in. This was a golden-faced young man who sported a permasmile and two dimples as deep as wishing wells.

"Can I help you, Miss?" He asked, as the French couple headed off to their room, barely able to keep their hands off each other.

What I thought was, *I'd like what they have.* What I said was, "I'd like to see the owner."

Smiley stopped smiling. "Is there something wrong with your room? Which suite are you in?"

"I'm not staying here. I mean, my, uh, colleague is, but I'm not."

"Is your colleague unhappy with the accommodations?"

"Not at all."

As if turned on by a remote switch under the counter, the smile came back. "Mr. Santos is very busy. Perhaps I can help?"

Now, if there is one thing I know, it is how to protect your king. I am a master of keeping the unworthy away from the prize, keeping the inner circle sealed shut. But part of that knowledge is the skill of reversing exclusivity. I am the reigning queen of infiltration.

I smiled warmly. "I'm an old friend, actually. I just dropped by to bring this to Nikos." I lifted the little white bag. "His favorite ice cream," I whispered, and punctuated with an inclusive giggle.

"O-oh!" The clerk sang, as though he'd just solved a clever puzzle. "You must be Isobel."

Isobel? Who the hell was Isobel?

"I'll just call him down." The clerk winked at me and picked up the Big Red Phone. "I just started here, so forgive me for not recognizing you." I nearly choked in a Pavlovian response to seeing the Big Red Phone in action again. "Miss Isobel is here to see you,

Mr. Santos," Smiley said into the phone. He paused and hung up. Strangely, he was no longer smiling. "He's just finishing some business. If you'd like to have a seat—"

"I'm not Isobel," I blurted. "My name is Norah Pasquale." I laughed lightly. "But about this Isobel. I'm curious, is she Nikos's—" It was no use getting more information out of the clerk; he was already on the BRP again.

"Don't bother, Martin. I'm right here," said a deep voice behind me.

He wouldn't have had to speak; the hairs on the back of my neck already knew it was Nikos Santos. I turned to face him, to try to explain, but I was stunned into stupefied silence by his sheer magnificence. No longer the Man in White, Nikos wore neatly-pressed navy trousers and a beige dress shirt with the top few buttons opened. His chestnut waves of hair were combed back, yet slightly tousled. He gave me one surmising glance then looked past me. A bludgeoning would have been kinder.

"This isn't Isobel," Nikos said calmly.

"My mistake," said Martin.

"Right. I'm Norah."

Martin spoke over me, as though I had magically disappeared. "She said she was an old friend. I just assumed."

Damn you, Smiley.

"An old friend," said Nikos, his dark eyes now glued on me as they had been that first terrible night. I felt my knees begin to gelatinize.

"Yes, well. I felt so badly about the last time we saw each other," I managed. "So, I brought you this." I took the pint of ice cream out of the bag and held it up. "Green tea ice cream? Your *favorite*?" God, I sounded like a mental patient. Nikos regarded it for a second. He turned straight around and headed toward the elevator. I was devastated. Speechless. Humiliated in front of Smiley Martin as well as several pairs of world travelers.

"Come on up," said Nikos over his shoulder.

It took a second for me to register what was happening. Nikos held the gate of the elevator open for me. My temples began to throb. *Move! Do something!* I sucked in a deep breath and took what I gauged would be a poised and elegant stride along the carpet toward his awaiting and open arms. Just like a fairy tale scullery-maid-turned-princess or an enchanting heroine in a Yash Chopra film. But very unlike either of those delightful scenarios, I lost consciousness before my foot even hit the ground.

The last thing I saw was a spray of melted green tea ice cream, airborne above plush burgundy carpet.

"I guess an ambulance brought me home. I don't know. I just woke up here."

Helen sat at the edge of my bed shaking down a thermometer.

"Ambulances don't bring you home, Norah. They bring you to the hospital."

"Well, whoever it was, I can't imagine how they knew where I lived or how they got in."

"I can," said Helen. "There's a phone bill and a set of keys sticking out of your purse."

I moaned. "Nikos must think I'm a complete putz."

"Nikos?" Helen raised an eyebrow.

"The Man in White. He's the owner of the hotel I checked Baz into that night you saved his butt."

"Ah, yes. Tell me about this Nikos."

"He's tall and beautiful and successful and self-assured. He doesn't walk, he glides—in a very masculine way, of course. He speaks softly yet firmly. And he's Italian! I mean he was born there, but he must have been raised here because he has no accent." I stopped myself. I was gushing. "Not at all my type."

"Well, he sounds perfectly edible."

"Oh, Helen," I wailed, pulling the covers over my head. "He's totally out of my league. When I stand next to him I look like I ought to be taking his brunch order."

"God, woman, were you raised under a staircase or something? Where did you get such low self-esteem?"

"This guy's different, Helen. I've already lost. Trust me. The first time I meet him, I piss him off. The second time I pass out and decorate his carpet with ice cream. We're hardly hitting it off."

Helen wrinkled up her nose. "True, you're starting out in a tough position. But you can use it to your advantage. Men love that quirky, falling down stuff. It appeals to their hero nature. It's cute. Very Bridget Jones."

I glared at her.

"Or Annie Hall, if you prefer the classics. Look, with just a little effort—"

"It doesn't matter. There's another woman."

"How do you know?"

"I told the clerk I was 'an old friend' and he gave me this weird look like I was talking in code. He thought I was someone named Isobel. If your employees know your personal visitors by name, that's got to mean something."

"Funny."

"What?"

"That name sounds super familiar."

From my purse came the tinkling of "I Can't Get No Satisfaction."

"You get it," I said, cocooning myself in the covers. "If it's Baz, tell him I'm too sick to play fetch today."

"Norah Pasquale's phone," Helen said, as sweetly as a wind chime. "Just a second." She pressed the phone to her chest and mouthed, "*It's Jason.*"

I shook my head. Helen gave a slow nod and handed me the phone.

"Yes?" I said, trying for a tone of perturbed aloofness.

"Norah, hi. Listen, I just wanted to apologize for the other night. I was really nervous and...I was an ass, okay? I want to make it up to you. How about dinner tonight?"

"Forget it, Jason."

Helen handed me a pad of paper on which she'd written: GET HIM BACK. I whispered to Helen, "I don't *want* him back," then spoke loudly into the phone, "You're a turd."

"Come on, Norah," pleaded Jason. "Give me another chance. I need you. You're my muse."

Helen handed me the pad again. She'd scratched out what she'd written and wrote: REVENGE. I smirked. It was obvious I wasn't going to be transcending my league anytime soon.

"You know what, Jason? Fine. One more chance."

"Excellent. How about El Arbol at eight?"

"See you at El Arbol." I clicked off.

"Spanish food, huh?" Helen said, already plotting. "That means hot, hot, hot outfit. Low-cut top, push-up bra. You'll look fabulous and you'll tell him all about your very successful new boyfriend who owns a chain of hotels."

"One hotel. And he's not my boyfriend. And I don't have big tits. That's three lies in a row. The karmic payback will be astronomical."

"Oh, like Jason's been so straight with you."

"That doesn't make it right for me to lie. I'd really rather just kneecap him."

"You gotta get that anger in check, girl. Boys don't like girls who talk like sailors."

"Thar she blows."

"I'm going to see what I have that might fit you," Helen said, ignoring me. "After tonight, he'll never look at another woman again."

"Does that mean part of the evening involves me blinding him with a butter knife?"

"Christ, do some deep breathing or something. I'll be right back."

Helen was so excited, I hated to let her down, but I doubted I would have the energy to hold my head up, never mind my mediocre bust. I got out of bed and turned on the computer.

Five emails. Junk spam. Three offered debt management programs, and one guaranteed I could make my penis three inches longer. I was about to delete them all, when the last one caught my eye:

From: *The Exchange*
Subject: *Your application*

My heart pounded into my ears. I clicked on it.

-----*Original Message*-----

From: Queen Bee <QueenBee@theexchange.com>
To: Norah Pasquale <norahnyc@hotmail.com>
Subject: Your application
Date: Wed, August 20, 11.59 pm

Thank you for your interest in The Exchange. We regret to inform you that your application has not been accepted.

Best of luck,
Isobel Marceau Santos

The sting of having been rejected from a stupid dating service was quickly overtaken by the crashing disappointment of seeing the third name in her signature. So she was Nikos's wife. Fine. But I wasn't about to let that smug little businesschick get away with rejecting me.

-----*Original Message*-----

From: Norah Pasquale <norahnyc@hotmail.com>
To: Queen Bee <QueenBee@theexchange.com>
Subject: RE: Your application
Date: Thu, August 21, 5.47 pm

Thank you for your interest in my "interest" in The Exchange. I regret to inform you, however, that my application was in jest. It is hard to believe that a woman as intelligent as I have been led to believe you are would waste her abilities creating what amounts to a sexist parlor game of deceit in order to help women find true love.

Therefore, your rejection of my application has not been accepted.

—NP

"Take that, 'Mrs.' Santos." I said as I clicked the send button.

Helen was a whirlwind of make-over madness. She was so caught up in my physical transformation that I couldn't bear to tell her about my rejection email, not to mention the discovery of Isobel's identity.

60

By the time she completed her project, Helen had cinched me up tight in one of her black suede corsets, which sat atop the satin tuxedo trousers I bought to attend the SAG Awards last year with Baz. She also lent me her Jimmy Choo strappy sandals and tweaked and flipped my hair to photo op perfection.

But there were no photographers at El Arbol. And by eight forty-five, it became increasingly clear that there would be no Jason, either. I leaned back in my chair and sipped my sangria.

"Mr. Fanking hasn't arrived?" The waiter asked cautiously. He looked like he was bracing himself for a tidal wave of loser girl tears.

"No, he hasn't." I spoke with a serenity befitting royalty. "However, I would like to finish my drink. Then I'd like you to bring the check."

"Very good," the waiter said, visibly relieved by my moxie.

"Oh, and if Mr. Fanking does finally arrive?"

"Yes?"

"Please tell him I left with someone very, very handsome."

The waiter beamed. "Most certainly, Miss."

"No, no, wait. Tell Mr. Fanking I have a new boyfriend, and I only came here tonight to let him down easy. And tell him my new boyfriend—who is very European and very gorgeous—owns a chain of successful hotels. And tell him—"

"Shall I get a pen?"

I slumped as far as the corset would let me. "No, forget it. Just tell him the first thing."

"You have a boyfriend."

"Yeah," I said, sadly. "That sounds good."

The Central Park Zoo was only a few blocks away from Jean-Francois, the upscale French spa on Madison Avenue where Helen worked as an aromatherapeutic esthetician. That means she made you smell good while removing your blackheads. Or something like that. As someone who barely has time for a shower, I never took much interest in the specifics of her career.

Helen met me on her lunch break wearing a white lab coat, which made her look more like my nursemaid than my best friend. We took our two plastic shells full of salad bar booty and sat at a table just outside the zoo gates. Helen had laid off about Jason's stand-up routine for a couple of days since it seemed every attempt she made to boost my spirits ended with me falling lower than I was before. But now she was giving me that look again. That look that was telling me to dust myself off and try again. Maybe she was my nursemaid, in a way. I avoided her eyes and concentrated on masticating my beets.

"I know I said I wouldn't ask, but did you ever get around to that, um, clothing website I showed you?"

"Yep."

"And?"

"Nope."

"Nope, what?"

"I thought you said we weren't supposed to talk about this outside of our own homes."

"We can talk in *code*," she said, as though it were the most obvious thing in the world. "What do you think the website front is for?"

"Okay. Uh, I must be out of fashion."

"Why?"

"No one wanted my clothes."

It took her a second to put it together. "You were *rejected*?" Helen asked, a little too loudly for my taste.

"Yes," I whispered. "I have now been rejected both by men and an organization of women who are looking to *find* men. That's why I've decided to become a nun and move to Calcutta as one of Mother Teresa's Missionaries of Charity."

"I think you have to be an actual Catholic first."

"Formality."

"I can't believe they rejected you."

"You mean *she* rejected me."

"You got an email from an actual person? That never happens. Because of the anonymity thing. It's usually from 'The Management' or something."

"I got a very short and decidedly not sweet email from one Isobel Marceau—"

"Ah!" Helen raised a triumphant arm in the air. "That's where I heard the name Isobel! The Exchange! Thank you. I was losing my freaking mind trying to remember."

"Wait. I didn't finish. Isobel Marceau *Santos*."

Helen lit a Capri. "Wow. What are the odds?"

"Whatever."

"But what about Nikos?"

My mind flashed on the sight of flying green tea ice cream. "Don't," I moaned. "I can't deal."

"Maybe Marceau is her middle name and she and Nikos are sibs."

I rolled my eyes and poked at Romaine strips with my white plastic fork.

"Then maybe they're divorced," Helen offered, hopefully.

"Hey, Nancy Drew? I don't give a shit. How's that?"

"Yes, you do. I see it on your face. You're sick in love with this hotel guy."

There was a slow burn rising from my chest to my esophagus, but that could have been from the marinated mushrooms. God knows how long they'd been sitting in that tray.

"I got it! I'll look Nikos up on the database for you! Maybe we can find out that way."

"Absolutely not," I blurted. "I don't want to know. Promise me you won't, Helen. Promise me."

"Fine," Helen said softly. "Jesus, you look like you're going to cry."

"I'm tired. That's all."

"Forget him then, Norah. I have someone better for you." Helen flicked an ash into her discarded chicken salad and pulled the *New York Times* from her bag. She pointed to a photo of a shortish, artsy-looking man standing in front of the Guggenheim. "This is Robin Fox."

"Cute. And thanks. But no."

"Why not, Norah? Get back on the horse. He's a real nice horse, too. Freelance art critic."

"Critics suck."

"You suck," said Helen with a pout.

I took the paper and gave his photo a closer look. Good posture. Nice dresser. He had kind of a "Most Interesting Man in the World" thing going on, which was entirely acceptable. Better than Nautica, anyway.

"How do I know he's not a psycho?"

Helen snuffed her cigarette out on the abandoned chicken chunks. "I used to date him a little."

"How little is a little?"

"A year. On and off."

"Helen! I'm getting your rejects now?"

"Relax. I gave Robin a good listing on the site. Meet him for the fun of it. No one said you have to marry him."

"I don't think nuns can get married."

"Don't move to Calcutta. At least until after the date."

"'The date' sounds awfully finalized, Helen. You didn't, by any chance, make a date for me without consulting me first, did you?"

Helen scooped up her lunch trash. "Look at the time, would you? I must dash, darling. But I will say this: American Art Coalition Gallery on Wooster Street, this Saturday, five o'clock. Casual dress. Kisses!"

I have never seen a woman bound up two fat sets of stone steps faster.

In the Line of Duty

"Quiet, please, for god's sake!" shouted Kevin, the despotic production assistant. It was only seven in the morning and already Kevin was red-faced and snapping at all the non-union background actors in his wake, with no shame for his unabashed rage. I liked Kevin.

Baz and I sat running lines in the bar where he was shooting. This was the scene where Captain Smithy would hear for the first time that two of his male officers were having an affair. "They're setting the stage for The Big News," Baz told me proudly.

The first hour or so they had a stand-in for him, to get the cameras and lights focused. All Baz had to do now was slip his little tush onto the bar stool and work his magic.

"We're ready for Mr. Vancouver," Kevin said. I took the tissues out of Baz's collar that were keeping the makeup off his shirt, and he stepped onto the set.

"Hi, everybody!" He said, waving. "Thanks for being awake this early. Lord knows I'm not." But the background folks were too paralyzed with The Fear of Kevin or the reality of being in Baz's presence that only a few grunted a nervous response.

Greg, the director, adjusted his Yankees cap in greeting. "You want a rehearsal, Baz?"

"Nah, let's do a take."

My little soldier.

"Okay, lock it up. Quiet on the set!"

"We have speed," said the sound guy.

"Fourteen-six," the clapper smacked in front of the camera.

"Background, and...*action.*"

"How long has this been going on, Lieutenant Harris?" asked Captain Smithy in his thick Queens accent, staring sternly into his Scotch (apple juice) glass.

"A few months now, Sir," I mouthed as the day player spoke his lines.

"What am I supposed to do about it? Call their mothers?" Captain Smithy slammed his glass down and spun toward Lieutenant Harris.

"The other officers are getting real uncomfortable about it, Captain. No one wants to back Jones and McKinney up anymore. They worry what the other guys'll think."

"Listen, Harris. I have a rash of mob hits making their way from SoHo to Central Park and I can't stop them alone. Ask the guys how comfortable they'll be when they're dead." Captain Smithy tapped the bar for another round. "They better get their priorities straight. Or I'll straighten them myself. Am I understood, Lieutenant?"

"Yes, Sir."

Smithy tossed back another apple juice and...

"Cut."

"Let's get a reverse angle. We'll go again in five." Greg said. "That was excellent, Baz."

Baz was beaming when he stepped back over to me. "You so rock," I said. "Can I have your autograph?"

"No, piss off," Baz smirked as Gina the make-up artist dabbed at his cheeks with a compact sponge. "Given any thought to my offer?" Gina gave a quick glance to my face that she probably thought was well disguised in nonchalance. "You might as well know, Gina," said Baz. "I've proposed to Norah."

"I heard," Gina said, incredulous. "Harriet told me."

"Right. What did I tell you?" Baz said. "The biggest mouth."

"So, it's true?" Gina dropped the sponge in Baz's lap.

"What do you think, Gina? Do we look like we're in love?"

Gina gave an exaggerated huff I wasn't quite sure how to take.

"I think that's fine, Gina," said Baz, handing her sponge back to her. "We'll send you an invitation."

"Really? Wow. Uh, thanks."

"You really shouldn't do that to nice people," I said, after she was a safe distance away.

"It's all in good fun," said Baz. "Besides, isn't it a thrill to have rumors circulating that you might actually be engaged to the rugged Captain Smithy?"

"Not rugged for much longer, huh? Not once they see you fall madly in bed with David Astor."

"Ah! Talking of. I need you to collect him at the airport."

"Sure thing. When does he arrive?

"Saturday. Half-past five."

"*This* Saturday?"

"We have a lot of research to do."

"Oh, is that what the kids call cruising gay bars nowadays?"

"Mr. Vancouver? Whenever you're ready," said Kevin, trying to come off relaxed. A vein struggled, near explosion, along the side of his temple. I hoped Kevin would live though the season.

When I got home that night, I had an email message from Isobel Marceau Santos, with the subject line: *Apology*. She requested my presence at her office to discuss an "error in judgment."

I laughed out loud. Did she think I was going to apologize to her just because I had an opinion? Granted, the perfect opportunity to find out if she and Nikos were married had just fallen in my lap. My stomach clenched tighter as I realized I was going to have to accept my fate and meet (the possible) Mrs. Santos face to face. If I didn't, I'd forever have that question burning my guts like battery acid.

If she was married to him, I'd back off. If not? Well, I shouldn't get ahead of myself. One goal at a time.

The message told me to meet her at the Millennium Conference Center in Times Square. Four o'clock, Saturday afternoon. Then it hit me. I had the Robin Fox date at five on Saturday. And I had to pick up David Astor at JFK at five-thirty. I'd have to give something up. There was no way in hell I was going to miss meeting Isobel now. And David Astor fell under the responsibilities of my job, after all.

I called Helen. "Wanna go work out?"

"There's nothing like sweating with strangers," Helen said as she poked the panel of the LifeFlex treadmill. We were at our favorite Midtown gym. It catered to a largely gay clientele, which meant that no one would ogle us in our jiggling spandex. It was worth the extra $200 a year.

"I have a dilemma." I stepped on my treadmill and started a leisurely stroll.

"I love dilemmas. As long as they're not mine."

"Actually, I have two dilemmas, but one is more impending than the other, so I'll start with that."

"Shoot," said Helen, beginning her jog.

"Three, really. I have three dilemmas."

"Slow down. I'm not Dr. Phil."

"I can't meet Robin on Saturday."

"Nothing doing. I'm not letting you chicken out, Norah. Robin's reviewing the gallery opening of this very hot Dutch artist. It's a big deal. Besides, I already told him you were coming and he's very excited."

"I have to work."

"Bullpoopy."

"No, I do. There's an actor coming into town for the show and Baz asked me to pick him up at the airport. You know how it is, Helen. I'm on call all the time. Like a doctor."

Helen grimaced and said nothing for almost five minutes. I picked up my pace on the treadmill. That went better than I'd expected.

"I'll go," Helen said, finally. A thin mist of sweat glistened on her forehead.

"To the opening? Great. Please tell Robin I'm sorry—"

"No, not the opening. I'll pick the actor guy up at the airport."

"You can't, Helen."

"What's the difference who does it? He'll get collected and dropped off and that's that."

"Because it doesn't look good. This is my job."

"Right, and I've never helped you out with your job before. I mean, it isn't like I risked my reputation to escort your famous boss out of our building in the middle of the night—"

"And I thank you for that. So does Baz. He's still in complete awe of your guile. But it was a special circumstance. Come on, Helen."

She slapped the STOP button of her treadmill and turned on me. "No, *you* come on. Over the last few years you have become an angry, lonely, workaholic. You do nothing positive for yourself. You say you want to fall in love, but you go into every possible encounter as though it's already doomed to fail. I swear, sometimes I think you sabotage your love life on purpose."

"Not on purpose," I said, almost inaudibly. I kept my eyes on the heart rate monitor in front of me, trying to block out the sudden image of Nikos's smoldering stare.

"Why won't you try harder to make something work with a man? You give up at the first little bump in the road."

"Like catching my boyfriend dry humping another woman in public and then apologizing for it by standing me up?"

Helen wiped her face with a towel. "Okay, that was in bad taste. But I bet you could have worked it out."

"He had his chance. You know, maybe I just haven't met anyone I wanted to put up with that much shit for, Helen. Have you thought of that?"

"Well, you're not *going* to find anyone if you keep spending all your time holed up with Bollywood rentals or getting yanked around like a pet poodle by Baz."

"Helen, this may be hard for you to understand, but I actually enjoy my life."

"I can see how happy you are."

"Yes, okay. I feel like a loser for not being able to keep a man in my life. But on the flip side, I really like not having to fluff myself up for dates, not having to answer to anyone—"

"Except Baz. You might as well be his wife."

I tripped and grabbed the handrails to steady myself. "Funny you should say that. Baz proposed to me the other day."

"Right. And I'm having one of Mick Jagger's love children."

"Not marriage. He wants me to be his full-time assistant. But I'd have to live in Los Angeles for half the year."

Helen's eyes widened. "You're doing it?"

"This is dilemma number two." Helen slapped my STOP button. I nearly fell flat on my face. "See, now that wasn't nice."

"Workout's over. We're going to Gilda's."

Eight years ago, Helen and I met for the first time at Gilda's, a neighborhood bar and grill two blocks from our apartment building. Helen was posting a notice for a roommate, and I was having a drink after spending all day apartment hunting. We lived together for a year, and when the apartment across the hall opened up, I took it.

Now we sat at our favorite table by the window for people-watching (and being people-watched), with easy access to the bar.

"Tell me," she said, sucking the straw of her vodka cranberry, "when are you going to L.A.?"

"I don't know that I am, Hel. I'm not sure I could stand being away from New York that long."

"But it's L. fucking A., you cow! Oh, my god. The glitz and glam and parties and restaurants."

"Yeah, you're right. New York has none of that."

"Trees, Norah! Palmy palm trees! And beaches!"

"We have trees and beaches. Anyway, I don't want to talk about it anymore. The whole thing makes my head hurt."

"What's number three?"

I took a quick swig of my Mimosa. "Is this some kind of a dirty riddle?"

"You said you had three dilemmas. What's the third one?" I sucked in a quick breath. "Norah? Is there a reason why you just turned completely red?"

"Oh, it's nothing. It's, um, about that clothing website."

Helen scrunched down and looked around to see if anyone could overhear us. "You changed your mind," she whispered. "You want me to look up Nikos on the database?"

"No, but I did get an email from our enigmatic Isobel today."

Helen's mouth fell open. "What did it say?"

"I wrote a not-so-nice response to my rejection and I think she wants me to apologize." Helen laughed. "My thoughts exactly. She wants me to come to her office."

The smile left Helen's face in a flash. "As far as I know, no one's ever met her. She's a fiercely private person."

"Well, I'm going to. Four o'clock on Saturday."

"Now you can find out if she's married to Hotel Boy."

"If it comes up. You know. No big deal. But I refuse to apologize to her. That's for damn sure." I sounded confident, strong. Good. Helen didn't have to know I was scared to death.

Helen leaned back in her chair. "And what about Robin?"

Maybe it would be good to have a date planned for immediately after I found out the man of my dreams was married. "I'll go," I sighed.

Helen's face lit up. "You will?"

"Yes, but please don't expect anything, okay?"

"No pressure, hon. But you'll just love each other. I know it." Helen ripped a corner off her napkin and took a pen out of her purse. "Now, tell me what I have to do to pick up this actor person."

"JFK. United Airlines. That's terminal seven. His plane gets in at five thirty-seven p.m." Helen was scratching away at the napkin. "You may wish to write this important information in a more permanent place." Helen looked at me quizzically. "You're not picking up your aunt from Miami, Hel. This is work. Be professional."

Without a word, Helen removed her daybook from her purse and creased it open to Saturday. She cracked her knuckles and began to transfer the information from the napkin to her book.

"Better," I said. She stuck her tongue out at me while she was writing. "I'll give you the number of the car service. All you have to do is go to the gate, hold up the sign with his fake name on it—"

"Fake name?"

"'Bleu'. It's our code for the show. He'll know. Now, when he arrives, just smile and greet him, and escort him directly to the car, which should be parked right outside the nearest exit. That's imperative. Then you go back in and get all his luggage sorted out to be sent to the hotel."

"To. The. Hotel," Helen said pointedly, as she wrote the words.

"Shit. I suppose I'll have to make a reservation for him at 'the hotel'."

"Ah, suck it up," said Helen. "I know you're dying to see Nikos again. You can't get anything past me, honey. I'm your best friend. That makes me clairvoyant." She tugged on her vodka-cran straw again. "Oh, what's this actor's real name, anyway? Am I allowed to know that much?"

"Oh, sorry. Of course. It's David Astor."

Helen put her pen down. She closed her eyes for a minute, then opened them. "I can't do it."

"What?"

"I cannot pick up—" Quick breath. "—*David Astor*—" Quick breath. "—from the airport."

"Why the hell not?"

"He's God."

"Helen, please."

"I'll make a fool of myself. Oh, shit. Does this mean David Astor is going to be on *Handsome Blue*?"

"That's what it means."

Helen gulped down the rest of her drink, bypassing the straw entirely. "David Astor is coming here. To my city. To be on my favorite show. David. Astor. Here."

"He's just a man, Helen. As they all are."

"He is not a man, Norah. He is David Astor."

"Will you please stop saying 'David Astor'?"

Helen clutched her chest. "He's not a *gay* man, is he?"

"Well, he'll play one on TV. Smithy's coming out and David's character is going to be his lover." I put my finger to my lips. "You didn't hear that from me."

Helen grasped the edges of the table with both hands. "My two favorite actors in the universe getting it on on national television? I'll never have to come up with another masturbatory fantasy as long as I live."

"You can tell him that when you meet him." I dropped some cash on the table.

"I can't. Seriously. I won't be able to breathe."

"You had no trouble meeting Baz."

"He's *gay*. No pressure."

"Actually, he claims to be 'ambisexual'. Or something. Look, it's fine. Don't worry," I said, pushing my chair back. "Just tell Robin I had to work, okay? I'm going home."

"I'm sorry I let you down, Norah," Helen said as we headed back to the apartment.

"Please, this is my job. Boring as it is sometimes."

"Boring? I don't think so. I have no idea how you do it. I mean, keep your cool around stars all the time."

I unlocked the front door and held it open for Helen. "They're just people, Helen. But when they're 'on'—you know, doing their celebrity thing—it's like they exist in a different world. I just watch it. Like a film. And when it's over, I go home. There's a difference between them and us, but then there's really no difference at all. Does that make sense?"

"Not really. But it sounded very Zen," said Helen.

Upon waking Saturday morning, a dull throbbing dread pervaded my entire body. I had already eaten two-and-a-half rolls of Tums by the time three-thirty rolled around. Helen came out of her apartment just as I left mine, wearing a flowered sundress and a determined smile.

"I'm going to the airport," she announced. "To get," she sucked in a breath and let it out, "David Astor."

"Are you sure? You look a little wobbly."

She nodded firmly. "I am going to meet David Astor—God, help me—and *you* are going to the gallery to meet Robin."

"Helen, you don't have to—"

She put up her hand. "I expect you to love me forever for this sacrifice and name your first three children after me. Now go. Quick, before I change my mind or wet myself or something."

When I arrived at the Millennium Conference Center, I was immediately approached by a young man in a suit.

"Mrs. Santos is waiting for you in the Harrington Suite," he said.

Mrs. Mystery solved. Shit.

The suited man wore a bright gold nametag, which I didn't read, since I kept hearing *Mrs. Santos* over and over in my mind like a Swiss Alps echo.

There was so much to do between this neutral spot at the desk and my eventual destination. I had approximately three minutes to press my clothes neatly against my skin, check my hair, breathe deeply, and remind myself that I am the most wonderful human being in the world, and if she can't see it, then screw her.

Suddenly, there I was, standing in front of the door to the Harrington Suite. I swallowed, lifted a fist to knock. The door clicked open to reveal a woman about my age and height, a little on the pudgy side, and primly dressed. Her face was efficiently made-up, her hair in a high, slicked ponytail.

Well. This was nothing! I could handle this. She was like the girls at my gym, the few there were.

"Isobel," I said extending my hand, congenially.

The woman looked at my hand then extended her own behind her, toward a door. "Mrs. Santos is in her office. I'm Claire, Mrs. Santos's assistant."

Lord, could everyone just stop saying "Mrs. Santos" before I put my fist through something?

"Nice to meet you, Claire." I doubted I was hiding my disappointment.

I followed Claire through the opulent conference suite and stood, fingering a gilded picture frame as she slipped in to see if Mrs.—Isobel—was "prepared to receive" me.

Give me a break.

Then the heavy white doors opened and there, behind an oak desk, stood the most beautiful woman I have ever seen.

Not beautiful. Exceptional. Striking. As in, just lie down and die because you will never know this kind of loveliness in your own skin. It was all I could do not to stare at her wide, green eyes and tawny silken hair. Her lips were luscious red, and slightly parted. Her body, a perfect play of curves and planes, was covered with a crisp pinstripe suit that was obviously tailored to her exact measurements.

She spoke her name—yes, *that* one—and extended a delicate ivory hand. I stepped forward and placed mine in hers. We both squeezed. Firmly.

"Please sit," she said, and did so herself.

I lowered myself into the leather seat and forced a few blinks, something I don't think I'd done since entering the room.

"I am sure you know what this is about," said Isobel. Now I noticed her accent. It was light, but very distinct. French.

Figured.

"I'm not sure that I do, actually," I said.

Isobel looked at me a moment, no expression registering on her face. Then she tilted her head toward Claire, who had been standing behind me, at the back of the room. "Claire, will you please see to the door?"

Was someone knocking? I didn't hear anything. Claire nodded and left. In a moment I heard a few beeps, like a security system. Claire had locked herself outside of the room.

Isobel took out a large file folder and opened it. She passed a piece of paper to me. It was my application. I scanned the document. Username, password, vital stats... Looked perfectly normal to me. Except, of course, for the big REJECTED stamp at the top.

"About this rejection," I began.

"It was nothing personal," said Isobel. "We filled our quarterly quota. There was simply no more room in the database. You can apply again in the fall."

What a let-down. "Well, then," I stood.

"Where are you going?"

"Aren't we finished?"

"No. I would like to ask you something," said Isobel with a faint smile.

"Now that you mention it, I have a question for you, too," I said.

"Please, you first."

"No, you."

Isobel shrugged and poured us both glasses of water from a crystal pitcher at the corner of her desk. I sat back down.

"When your application was rejected, your response was heated, to say the least. You called this organization, what was it?" She lifted another sheet from the file and read aloud. "'A sexist parlor game of deceit'." Isobel paused. "You know, I created The Exchange to assist women in the difficult process of finding a mate in a modern metropolitan city. There are many who would be lost without it. I wonder, Norah, if you truly feel this way about my organization, why did you bother applying in the first place?"

I opened my mouth to speak at least three times before I realized there was nothing that sounded right. Except one thing.

"I'm sorry."

Perfect. The one thing I promised myself I wasn't going to say.

Isobel smiled warmly. "You have not answered my question."

I saw it clearly now. She brought me here to torture me mentally. Fine. Best to give her the truth and get out. I cleared my throat. "I applied because my dear friend, who is an active member, suggested it. She knew I was tired of playing games, doing that dance we do just to get a man. But I suppose it's just something we have to do. Sure, we all have the fantasy of foresight, but isn't part of the fun of relationships getting to know someone?"

"This knowledge takes time. A lot of career-driven women do not have that kind of time to play around."

"If they're that driven, maybe they shouldn't be looking for mates."

"And you wish to make that decision for all the women in Manhattan." Isobel's voice was measured, relaxed. She was obviously two steps ahead of me, batting my mousy little self around like the cat she was.

I felt my blood pressure rising. If she had been anyone else, she would have been the recipient of one of my famous toxic wordstorms. And I'd probably hurl that pretentious crystal pitcher against the wall just to make my point.

I took a deep breath, mirroring her calm. "Look, I appreciate your time. I assure you The Exchange is safe. My lips are sealed. I accept your rejection, and now I have to go." I stood and headed for the door.

"Where?"

I spun around with the words "none of your business" on my tongue, but what came out was, "I have a date."

Isobel and I both began to laugh.

"Please come back," she said with a sincerity that made it impossible for me to refuse. "You have not let me finish." Isobel turned to her computer and punched a few keys. "Your rejection has been retracted."

"What about the quarterly quota thing?"

"I am the boss. I can do whatever I want. Come," said Isobel. "I want to show you something."

I stepped around the side of the desk and sat on its edge, peering over Isobel's shoulder at her computer screen. She smelled faintly of tuberose. She typed the name Jason Fanking into The Exchange's search engine.

"This is the man you sent us in your application."

I nodded.

"See this icon?" she said, pointing to a pair of red lips. "That means he is a good kisser. At least according to 'LateNiteLady'. Would you agree?"

"I suppose," I said, absently. "What does that mean?" I pointed to a skull and crossbones.

"It means, Norah, that he cheats."

I felt strange, all of a sudden, as though I were reading Jason's private medical records. I went back to my chair on the other side of the desk, but I didn't sit.

"There is something else you should know," Isobel said, noticing my discomfort. "This database is not only for convenience. It can protect women as well. There are some men listed here who are red-flagged."

"Red-flagged?"

"It means we have assigned the icon of a red pennant to their names. These men are, for all intents and purposes, off limits to other members of The Exchange." She typed another name and hit return. "Like this one."

I leaned forward and read: NIKOS SANTOS.

Oh, god.

"The owner of the Hotel Ursula." Isobel said quietly. "Which I noticed was also your password."

I had a hot flash that I attempted to mask by smoothing a casual hand over my hair.

"Have you stayed there?" Isobel asked.

I waited until I could control my voice. "Someone I know is staying there."

Isobel raised a cool eyebrow. "Did you know that this very conference center and Hotel Ursula are owned by the Santos family?"

"Really. How interesting. Isn't Santos your last name, too? Same family?"

Isobel made a little *hm* noise.

I swallowed. "So why is he red-flagged?"

"A man can be red-flagged for any number of reasons. Perhaps he is a cheater, like your Jason. Or maybe he is violent." Isobel took a small sip of her water. "Or perhaps there is a woman who cannot bear to share him."

My hands went clammy. "May I ask you my question now?"

"Certainly."

"Did you start The Exchange because of a man?"

She gave a small shrug. "Like you, I got tired."

"You didn't answer my question."

Isobel smiled up at me with languid, sea-green eyes. "Yes. I did."

"Was it because of Nikos Santos?" I licked my lips, but my tongue was dry.

Isobel shook her head, but it wasn't a *no*, necessarily. More of a refusal to answer my question. "All you need to know, Norah, is that this man hurt me."

The way she pressed the word *hurt* made me think that perhaps something else besides her heart had been broken. I stood there a moment. Isobel straightened suddenly and took a cleansing breath.

"I do not want to make you late for your date," she said, extending her hand again. "I hope you will consider sharing your experiences with The Exchange."

"I'll think about it," I said.

"Just remember." Isobel's hand was firmly in mine. "Red-flagged men are strictly off-limits. We women have to look out for one another, no?"

"Absolutely."

I headed straight downtown to the gallery, only stopping for a slice of Joe's pizza and a quick phone call to Helen to be sure she was safely JFK-bound.

"Everything all right?"

"Yeah, I only threw up twice."

"Where are you?"

"In the car. Hang on. *Terminal seven*," she said to the driver and got back on the line. "Oh! How was your meeting? Is Isobel a total troll?"

"The most ravishing troll I ever saw."

"Shit. Did you find out if she and Nikos—"

"Not for sure. But get this: It *was* a man who got her started on the whole Exchange thing. She said she got hurt. She showed me Nikos in the database. Red-flagged."

"Big surprise. Bet it was him."

"I doubt it."

"Why?"

"The guy she described sounds like some brute of a man with a temper like Tyson."

There was a moment of staticky silence. "And why can't that be Nikos?"

"I can't imagine him hitting a woman. He's so—"

"Italian."

"What does that have to do with anything? He's Tony Soprano now?"

"My advice is stay out of it. Too risky. They probably have one of those obsessive love-hate things. Like in a Polanski film."

I flashed on an image of Nikos and Isobel locked in a naked embrace, covered in bruises and kisses. Their combined beauty could short out the planet. I stopped walking for a second to fend off a wave of tears.

"Robin, on the other hand," continued Helen, "is nice English stock. Very courteous and clean."

"You can stop selling him," I said, trying not to sound sniffly. "I'm fifty feet from the gallery."

"Have a good time. Did you bring condoms?"

"Did you?" More silence, then what sounded like muffled choking. "Are you puking in the car? That's not professional, Helen."

"There's nothing left in my stomach," Helen said hoarsely. "But I think I just broke a blood vessel in my eye, so you can bet David Astor will fall in love with me at first sight."

"Helen, listen to me. You are not a call girl. You're not there to pick him up."

"Yes, I am."

"Right. Pick him up and *drop him off*..." It hit me. "...at the hotel where he has no reservation because I never made one. Shit!"

"Call them," said Helen. "It's probably better if you don't see that Nikos guy again, anyway."

"You're right," I admitted.

"No, I'll call," said Helen. "Might as well, since I'm all about David Astor today." She gave a little moan.

"Hey, do you want a trick you can use? It's something I used to do when I first started out and I was still a little starstruck around Baz."

"Anything is better than dry heaving."

"Imagine wiping his butt."

Silence.

"Feel better?"

"Much. And I'm pretty sure I'll never be able to have sex again."

Inside the gallery were several people wandering around several other people, except that half the people were made of plaster. The people-sculptures were posed to be attending a gallery opening, so as the live art patrons regarded the statues, the statues were regarding them. There were video projections on the walls of still more people wandering through an art gallery.

Robin appeared from behind a pressurized wall, behind which, I assumed, was more of the show. I recognized him from the newspaper photo. He looked much more handsome in real life. He held a digital recorder in one hand and glass of white wine in the other. When he saw me, he pocketed the recorder and shook my hand.

"Norah? Robin Fox. I hope you don't mind, I got started before you arrived. Thought I'd get some of the work part done so we could enjoy ourselves."

"No, it's fine." I felt like I was on an independent study field trip for college.

"Have you met the artist, Daag? I was just doing a quick interview. Let me introduce you."

Robin took my elbow and led me behind the wall. This area was much darker, with indigo walls. Besides being the place where the Chardonnay and Brie were laid out, I didn't see any artwork at all.

"Daag," Robin said to a husky blonde man we'd stopped in front of, "this is Norah Pasquale." Robin said my name as though it were a gourmet entrée. "Norah, Daag Framjen."

"Eh, what's up, Daag?" I put out my hand. "Sorry. I couldn't resist."

"It's all right," said Daag. "When I first came to America I didn't understand what was so funny. Someone had to tell me. Bugs Bunny doesn't translate the same in Dutch."

"What do you think?" Robin asked, handing me a cup of wine.

"I just got here, so I'm going to have a look around, if that's all right?"

"Of course."

"Is this room part of the show?"

Daag smiled broadly and pointed to the ceiling. It appeared to be an aquarium, fully stocked with tropical fish and plant life.

"Ohhh," I said, breathily. "That's amazing. Are they okay up there?"

"Perfectly safe," said Daag, looking up. "As long as the glass doesn't break."

I slipped out and back into the people-watching-people room. After a moment, the video projections on the walls made it very difficult to discern who in the room was real and who wasn't. That was most likely the reason I backed directly into Nikos Santos.

Of course, he didn't realize it was me; by the time he turned around, I'd already said my perfunctory "excuse me," realized who he was, and leapt behind the nearest plaster statue, which thankfully happened to be a fat woman carrying a poodle. I could still feel the quick pressure of his back against mine as I crouched there, holding my hands together to keep them from shaking.

Of all the galleries in all the towns in all the world...

Safely ensconced behind the fat statue's hip, I watched Nikos. He was dressed in a neatly pressed white cotton shirt and soft, chocolate brown trousers. A perfect choice for the weather and the event. I wondered if he had a personal dresser.

Nikos appeared to be alone. No one was around him now as he reached out to touch the cheekbone of a female statue that was doing the same to him. I was only one step away from my hiding place when I saw Daag heading right toward us. I slid myself back behind the fat woman. "Please, please, please don't see me," I prayed silently.

"Nik! You're here!"

I peered underneath the statue's armpit in disbelief. Nikos and Daag were in a tight bear hug. Nikos released him and grasped Daag's shoulder. "How could I miss your first U.S. show?"

"Good space, yah? Not like that hole in Paris. Remember?" Nikos wrinkled his brow and nodded in empathy. "Speaking of, how is Isobel?"

"Speaking of that hole in Paris?"

"Oh, my. No. I'm still working on the English idioms."

Nikos smiled a little. "She's all right, I suppose. Still running her fashion website out of Alexis's space."

"And you're all right with that?"

Nikos shrugged. "You know Iz. I can't tell her anything."

He calls her Iz. He tries to tell her things. I rested my head against the statue's ample bosom, and tried not to whine audibly.

"How's the show going?"

"Excellent," said Daag. "I've already made friends with the *New York Times* critic and his girlfriend."

I whined audibly.

"That's my boy. Where are they?" Nikos said, swiveling around. "I want to tell them how wonderful you are. Not that you need my help."

My heart raced. I had to get out. I made a break for the back of the room, but was instantly nabbed by Robin, who I hadn't seen standing a few feet behind me.

"Fun room, huh?" he said, sweetly. "Daag's calling us over. Come on."

"No," I said, too quickly. "I, uh, have to use the ladies' room."

"Catch up with us when you're done."

"Sure thing," I said.

Robin put a friendly hand on my back to point me in the direction of the toilets. I wished he hadn't done that. Out of sheer instinct, I glanced behind me to see if Nikos noticed the touch.

Sure enough, Nikos was looking right at me. When he saw me his expression went from smiling, to confusion, to recognition, then back to a very different sort of smile. I swallowed hard and bolted for the bathroom.

If people were asking Nikos about Isobel, they must be a couple. I splashed cold water on my face. It made perfect sense. How beautiful and classy they both were. How perfectly sophisticated and self-possessed.

Here's what happened: They fought, he hit her, she left, he confessed his love, she came back then ditched him. She started a secret website to get clandestine revenge and red-flagged her man to be sure no other woman could have him. As far as I know, it's gone on like this for years. Helen was right; I needed to stay out of it. Barring my digital expeditions into Hindi Fantasyland, obsessive, eternal love was way out of my frame of reference. It was all I could do to get a third date.

I sat in one of the stalls for several minutes, playing out the possible scenarios for a quick escape. Sure, the adult thing to do would be to go out there and be gracious and witty. But that would involve grace and wit, something I could not seem to muster in the presence of Nikos Santos.

There was plenty of time to psychoanalyze it later—and I would, probably for hours and hours—once I was tucked away safely at home. Right now, my only concern was getting myself out with as little disruption as possible.

Just outside the ladies' room door was a group of chatting women. I blended in with them as well as I could while scoping out the gallery floor. Luckily, Robin was standing right by the exit. Daag and Nikos were nowhere to be seen.

"Robin. Sorry," I said after making my way over to him.

"Are you all right?"

"I'm kind of feverish. I think I need to go."

"No problem. But why don't you wait it out?"

"Wait what out?" My voice quavered like a pubescent boy's.

Robin cocked his head toward the front door. "Have you taken a look outside? Torrential downpour. Out of nowhere. Looks like we've hit monsoon season."

"Fantastic."

"Let me call you a cab."

"No, no. I have a car," I lied. "It was, uh, nice to meet you."

Once outside, I was so happy to be free, so happy not to have fallen down or passed out or screamed at anyone or broken anything, that it took three whole blocks before I realized I now had dripping hair, mascara-streaked eyes, and clothes that clung to me as though they'd been superglued there. Clothes that were now also nearly transparent. By Bollywood standards, I was ripe for hero-pickin'.

I crossed my arms over my braless chest and stepped off the Houston Street curb just as a silver Mercedes pulled around the corner and slammed to a stop just inches from my toes. I brought a fast fist down against the hood. "Watch yourself, asshole. You almost hit me!"

The passenger side window lowered. I poked my head in to give the idiot driver the rest of my tongue-lashing, but froze before I could speak a word.

Nikos Santos was behind the wheel, peering at me over the rims of amber-tinted sunglasses. "We have to stop meeting like this," he said. "What will people say?"

I stood and held myself tighter. Suddenly, all I could envision was Isobel pawing at Nikos's tanned and hairy chest as he punished her with kisses.

"Come on, I'll give you a ride."

"Nuh," I managed. "B'thanks."

I started walking away in the wrong direction. Nikos was watching; it was too late to turn back. Hot rain water pelted my face, encouraging what I knew was coming. I didn't try to stop it; I let a few tears of frustration mingle with the rain. The Mercedes edged alongside me then stopped abruptly.

"Get in the car," said Nikos, sharply. The verbal equivalent to a quick slap in the face.

I got in the car.

Nikos reached over toward my leg. I nearly jumped through the sunroof glass. He gave me a curious look before clicking the glove compartment open. A box of tissues presented themselves.

I dragged a couple of them over my face. They came away black with mascara. Great. What did it matter, anyway? He already had the most beautiful woman in the city. Driving me home was obviously some act of pity like giving a street kid your gloves when it's snowing out. Who needed that kind of treatment? Certainly not me, despite my current urchin-like appearance.

"Don't you want to know where I live?" I asked, hotly.

"I know where you live."

I sagged in the leather seat. "Oh, god. It *was* you."

"Do you have any idea how expensive it is to remove green tea ice cream from Persian carpeting?"

"No, no. Please stop. I'm so sorry—" I turned to Nikos. He was smiling.

There was gray in his hair, just a few streaks at the temples. In an instant, I was lost in his face. It was so peaceful. Beatific, even. Helen must have been wrong; how could a man with a face like that ever do harm to another human being?

I broke off my gaze and concentrated on the ascending streets along First Avenue. "So," I said, "How do you know Daag?"

"I used to be his dealer."

"His dealer. As in—"

"Heroin."

"Ah."

Nikos laughed. "His art dealer. In Paris."

"What happened?"

"My mother died and left my brother and me her hotels." Nikos took a pack of Marlboros from his pocket and lit one. "Someone had to run them." He held the pack out to me.

I stared at it. The sweet little family of cylindrical siblings, all nestled together. There was one peeking out of the crowd, practically begging, "Take me. I was made for you." I could just slide its cool firmness from the pack and place it between my lips, tongue the spongy tip before I lit the other end and took a hot, biting pull...

"Thanks. But I quit."

Nikos fingered the perky cigarette back down with the others and re-pocketed the pack. "Do you mind?"

"No, I like it. My best friend smokes. Sometimes I make her blow it in my face."

Nikos smiled at me. "What about you?"

"Smoking makes me angry. At least I think it's the smoking. All the chemicals?"

"I meant did you meet Daag through your boyfriend?"

"Sorry. My what?"

"He's a critic for the *Times*, right?"

"No, he isn't. I mean, he *is* a critic for the *Times*, but he's not my boyfriend. Robin was a blind date. My smoking girlfriend's ex. How sad is that?"

"Not at all. It's hard to meet people in this city."

"We don't seem to be having any trouble. Wherever I go, there you are."

"I have to ask you, Norah." Nikos looked over at me. "Why green tea ice cream?"

"Because it's your favorite?"

He shook his head.

"The website said—"

"What website?"

"The website for your hotel. I was, uh, doing research, you know, for Baz."

"Baz."

"Vancouver. The actor. In the Presidential Suite. My boss? Registered as Charles Skye—"

"Yes, I remember," said Nikos, his eyes on the road.

"Anyway, I saw that it said your favorite food was green tea ice cream, so it seemed like a good way to make peace after that horrible—"

"Typo," said Nikos, cryptically.

"What?"

"On the website. There should have been a comma between 'green tea' and 'ice cream'. Two separate things. I like green tea. And I like ice cream. Hazelnut, if you're keeping track."

"I see." I hung my head. Droplets of rain abseiled from ropes of hair and plonked on the gray leather seat. "Well, that's perfect."

He pulled up to my building and stopped the car. My hand was already on the door.

"It's all right," Nikos said softly. "It was sweet."

"Oh, yeah? You licked it off the floor?" I huffed.

"No." He placed his hand on my knee. This time I did not flinch. "It was sweet of *you*."

I looked down at his hand until he removed it, then I got out of the car. "You know," I said before shutting the door, "Contrary to your experience with me thus far, I do know how to handle myself in public, how to speak and move and act. But for some dumb reason every time I'm around you, I—"

Nikos waited patiently for me to finish. His shirt had gaped open and I could see the left side of his chest, moving up and down slowly with his breath.

Red-flag. Off-limits. Back off. I felt the tears begin to ping my face again.

"Thanks for the ride," I said, and slammed the door shut.

"Perhaps he was kidnapped," said Baz on the other end of the phone. "I came back from dinner, went to the front desk to get David's room number, and they said he wasn't in. Don't know what could have happened between you picking him up at JFK and getting him to the hotel. Perhaps he joined a cult. Or got swept away in a tornado á la Dorothy Gale. All I know for sure is that one of the biggest celebrities of our day is now a missing person. Why might that be, Norah?"

I had made the mistake of getting directly into a hot bath and not checking on the completion of Helen's task. Now I was up to one ear in bubbles and up to the other in the ranting of my perturbed boss.

"Calm down. What do you mean he's not there? Maybe he went out for a walk or something."

"Norah, I'm telling you, he *never checked in.*"

I bolted upright and sent a tidal wave of tubwater over the edge of the porcelain. "That's not possible," I said, mostly to myself.

"Well, did you pick him up or didn't you?"

"I didn't," I said, wincing. "But Helen did. I had an appointment. Please don't hate me."

There was no sound on Baz's end of the line. He hated me.

I heard the clinking of ice in a glass. "Later," said Baz in a forced calm I had never before heard from him, "when this is all sorted out, you can tell me when this little Tom Sawyer kick of yours started. But now—really, Norah, getting your friends to do the work I entrust, not to mention *pay* you to do! It's not like you."

I sank further into the tub. "Baz, I—"

"Just find David. We have a breakfast meeting with Greg tomorrow at eight."

"Eight."

"That's in the *a.m.*, Norah."

"I am aware that morning is when a breakfast meeting is usually scheduled. Don't be rude, Basil."

"Call me when you've fixed this mess," Baz said, then clicked off.

No question Baz was a diva, but before today I'd never had those feline claws turned on me. I felt slimier than before I got in the tub.

There was no answer when I phoned Helen—home phone or her cell. I got out of the tub, dried and dressed myself. On my way out of the apartment, I grabbed Helen's spare keys. I wouldn't use them unless I had to.

Three sets of increasingly loud poundings on her front door roused no response from inside.

Don't panic, I told myself. *She's fine. He's fine. You'll find out very soon that everybody's fine. And* then *you can kill her.*

I pounded one more time, this time yelping frustrated obscenities in between the injustices of Helen letting me down on one goddamned favor that even a half-witted robot could do, when the door to my left opened.

Mrs. Garibaldi. The oldest living woman in Yorkville. And, not coincidentally, the deafest. I must have really been pounding hard for her to come outside, as she was now, in her dressing gown, holding a wooden spoon. Presumably for defense.

"Madon'," she said, waving the spoon at me. "Such a yelling. You all right?"

"Yes. Sorry, Mrs. Garibaldi. I know it's late."

"You own the state?" she asked, squinting.

"Jesus Christ, why me?" I shook my head. "I'm looking for Helen."

"You keep cursing against God, you find hell soon enough."

"Hel-*en*," I said, louder, pointing to Helen's front door. "I knocked, but I can't hear anything."

Mrs. Garibaldi nodded her comprehension then shrugged. "I don't hear nothing." She lowered her spoon and went back inside.

"I realize that, you incredibly helpful woman," I said to Mrs. Garibaldi's closed door.

I went back into my apartment and called the car service. The manager assured me that car 282 had collected David Astor at JFK's terminal seven and dropped him off at his hotel.

"Which hotel?" I was grasping for any possible mix-up that could have occurred.

"I'll have to check the name, but the drop-off address was 84th and Third."

That was this address.

"Are you sure that wasn't the original pick-up location?"

"Lady, I'm doing this job fifteen years. I know my own order slips. Drop off was at six forty-five tonight. Corner of 84th and Third."

I swallowed. "How many people?"

"One."

I clicked the phone off and fingered Helen's spare keys in my pocket. I headed back to Helen's door and quietly unlocked the deadbolt and the main door lock. The apartment was dark.

"Helen?" I whispered. "Don't freak. It's Norah."

There was no response. Something felt off. I crept back toward her bedroom, steeling myself for what I imagined would be some gruesome sight. Helen may have short-circuited and dumped

David off on the highway, then come home and dry-heaved herself to death from the guilt.

I flicked on the hallway light and peered into her bedroom. She was in bed. Thank God she was safe, but that didn't get me any closer to finding out where David Astor was. I took a small step into the bedroom, and saw a mound of *something* in Helen's bed. Just then, I heard the front door open, so I grabbed the closest thing I could lift—which happened to be a faux Oscar statue I'd given Helen for her 35th birthday—and held it like Casey at the Bat.

"What the shit, Norah?" Helen said, flicking on the kitchen light. She put two bags of groceries down on the counter.

I raced to Helen, covered her mouth with my hand and backed her against the wall. "Shh! There's someone in your bedroom," I whispered.

Helen shook her face away from my hand. "Relax, Cagney. I *know*. Man, you scared the bullpoopy out of me."

"I scared *you*? Do you have any idea how worried I was? And where is David? What did you do with him?"

Helen patted me on the head as she passed, heading toward the bedroom. We stood together in the doorway of her darkened room, staring in at the lump lying on her bed. Helen sighed dramatically.

"David Astor," she whispered, "is awfully tired from the jetlag—"

"It's three hours—"

"—and from all the fucking in the limo."

"You didn't."

"Oh, yes. Yes. Yes. Yes."

"But the guy at the car service said only one person was dropped off."

"I gave David the keys to my place, then I got out at the Food Emporium," Helen said, heading back to the kitchen. "David's going to be famished when he wakes up."

"What happened to my advice about being professional, Helen? What about the butt-wiping imagination thing?"

"I tried that." Helen removed a jar of pasta sauce out of a shopping bag. "Turns out it didn't bother me. In fact, if it came to it, I wouldn't mind. Kind of like *Kiss of the Spider Woman*."

"Christ."

"I'm in love." Helen sighed and unpacked some garlic and fresh basil. "Want to stay and eat with us?"

"I have work to do," I said, peppy as a deflating balloon.

"Loser."

"Bitch."

"Will you try to be happy for me?"

Plastering a big fake smile on, I spoke through my teeth. "See how happy I am?"

"Yeah, thanks." Helen stopped me before I got to the door. "Oh! What happened with Robin?"

For a moment I had no idea who she was talking about. "Robin. Right. Well, Nikos happened to be at the gallery opening, so I feigned illness and vamoosed, directly into a rainstorm."

"Shit."

"Wait, it gets better. Then Nikos happened to pull up in his car, so I got in and he drove me home."

Helen dropped the head of lettuce she was holding. "Did you?" She gasped. "Is he *here*?"

"Some of us have self-control."

"Not nice."

"I'm not feeling very nice."

"Well, maybe if you—" Helen grabbed the counter and ground her hips into it a few times.

"Humped the kitchen counter? Seriously, Hel. Nikos is a Red Flag Man. Besides, even if he wasn't, I don't want to get involved in that thing he has going on with Isobel. No good can come of it."

"Loser."

"Bitch."

"Cool, cat fight." David stood in the hallway, shirtless, rubbing the sleep from his face.

Helen bounded across the room and into his arms. "Davey! This is Norah."

"Hey, Norah. Baz told me all about you. He said you're the best."

For the first time in years, I was actually starstruck. I could hardly believe I was standing in the presence of a Hollywood demi-god and his naked torso.

"David Astor," I muttered. "Wow."

"Now you *have* to stay and eat with us," said Helen.

All through the meal, I kept my head bowed to my plate and pictured wiping David Astor's behind. I skipped dessert.

Getting Back on the ~~Hotel~~ Horse

Helen swore me to secrecy about her "David thing." Nearly a month had gone by, and from the late-night scufflings and giggles coming from the hall—and the fact that I hadn't seen much of my best friend after that pasta dinner—it seemed the "David thing" was getting serious.

Since David was in such high spirits, Baz had forgiven me for my negligence. I redoubled my efforts to be a good assistant. Now that I had the confirmation that Isobel was indeed connected to Nikos, I thought it would be an easy task to return to my old, loner life as though nothing had happened.

It was. For approximately five days.

I wanted so much to find out more about Nikos and Isobel, their love. Mostly, I wondered why I never had anything so passionate as that in my life. Besides my nightly Hindi romance films, the most passion I'd seen lately was coming from the scenes Baz and David were rehearsing as they developed their television love affair.

For days, I sat in Baz's suite with the two of them, nibbling incessantly off the complimentary fruit baskets room service kept sending up while the two of them ran lines and practiced balancing cop machismo body language with the foreshadowing of deep love to come.

Most of the time I was numb to it. Over and over, I saw David touch his prop gun or hold a pen, then stop at Baz's impatient *Cut*! "Do it again," he'd say, "with more tenderness. As though you really wish it was me you were touching."

"Or Helen," I wished I could say. But of course, I didn't.

Luckily, I never ran into Nikos. The first few rehearsal dates I slinked around, eyeing every corner, muttering prayers to the gods and goddesses that Nikos was away on business. After consistently not seeing him, I began to believe my prayers had been answered.

David's first appearance on the show was the following week, so rehearsals had doubled in frequency as well as intensity. One afternoon, I crossed the lobby on my way up to Baz's suite—with Baz's favorite Baklava and David's Evian in tow.

"Norah."

I turned around to see Isobel's assistant, Claire, sitting in one of the lobby chairs, staring intently at her mobile phone as though it were a mirror. On the table in front of her were several pages of an intricate-looking spreadsheet.

"Claire, isn't it?" I asked, politely. "What brings you here?" A question I knew the answer to, but wished I didn't.

Claire pointed with an elegant silver stylus pen toward the elevator I was just about to board. "Isobel's here. She's," Claire gave a little smile, "visiting someone."

"Oh," I said as non-chalantly as possible. "Nice hotel, huh?"

Claire blinked. "And you? Visiting, too?" She nodded toward the bag in my hand.

"No," I said. "I'm here on business." I lifted the bag: "For my clients."

There was an uncomfortable silence, during which I tried to block out of my mind the one question I wanted to ask Claire and replace it with some other pleasantry to end the conversation and get the hell out of there. But the more I thought about what I didn't want to say, the less I could formulate any other sentence.

"Well!" I said far too jovially, "Tell Isobel I said hello. Or maybe I'll see her myself. In a corridor or something."

"Doubt it," said Claire, turning back to her work. "I don't think there are any corridors up where she is."

"Yes. Well. Bye, then."

Claire raised her pen again as I walked, leadfooted, toward the elevators. As they clacked shut, I pressed the floor for the Presidential Suite. Involuntarily, my free fist began to clench and unclench.

No corridors? What did that mean? What part of a hotel didn't have a blessed corridor? Was Isobel leaping from balcony to balcony for sport? I stared meditatively at the illuminated button I had just pushed. Second from the topmost button, the one that read PH.

The Penthouse.

Of course.

Before I realized it, my finger was hovering over the button. Scenario Number One: The doors open on the penthouse and I'm face-to-face with a security guard who demands to know my name. There was probably another Big Red Phone up there. Bad news.

Scenario Number Two: The doors open directly on the penthouse living room, where Nikos and Isobel are engaged in kinky sexplay that involves leather and overripe figs. I'd have to buy my way out of it with Baklava and Evian, which could actually work. But what a ridiculous idea: Any idiot could just press the PH button and arrive smack in the middle of Nikos Santos's living room? No, that would have been very poor planning on the architect's part.

Scenario Number Three: The doors don't open at all. Didn't you usually need a special key to get to the penthouse? But there wasn't a keyhole next to the button.

Then again, I could always press PH, but just get off at the Presidential Suite. Unless there were hidden security cameras somewhere or freelance forensic teams doing spot checks on the place, no one would ever know.

I pressed PH.

The floors continued to pass slowly, clacking in a comforting rhythm. The car jerked to a stop at Baz's floor.

Make an effort!

Helen's words suddenly screamed in my ear. I put a hand on the gate door.

Stay out of it. Too risky.

Wise advice. But then a flood of other Helen gems began battling it out in my brain.

Lonely workaholic!

Try harder!

Loser!

I yanked open the elevator gate, dropped the bag outside the suite doors, and knocked twice. David opened the door, looked down at the bag, then up at me as I slammed the gate shut. He was wearing Baz's bathrobe. I made a mental note to mull that one over later.

"Everything okay?" he asked.

"I'll be right back. I just...forgot something."

"But the elevator's going up."

"Oh. Is it?" I slammed the gate shut.

In my estimation, walking into a Roman Polanski film starring Nikos Santos and Isobel Marceau Santos would be the best antidote for all my fantasizing. What I needed was a good, solid, in-your-face image of two disgustingly beautiful human beings engaged in soul-consuming sexual intercourse.

Or, Scenario Number Four: A post-coital screaming match. That would work just as effectively. I walk in on the two of them half undressed, their hair still damp from sweat. He's in the process of making a fist—curling together with fury the very same fingers that had, moments before, been inside her with love.

Yes, that would just about do it for me. With an image like that stuck in my mind, I would never ever delude myself again that that caliber of passion had any business in my reality. I'd leave them alone forever and return for good to my life of smartly-dressed art critics, stand-up cheaters, and pretty Bollywood boys.

To my surprise, the elevator door opened on a medium-sized foyer that was decidedly bereft of any snarling security guards. There were two white doors in the center of the wall, each with matching golden handles.

I couldn't risk getting trapped up there, so I removed the DKNY pump from my right foot and propped the elevator door open with it. Crouching in front of the white doors with my ear pressed to the crack in between them, I could make out two distinct voices. Nikos's was for certain, but the second... I had to be sure it was Isobel.

"I want to set things right," the deep voice said. "I just don't know how."

Nikos. Definitely. I pushed my head so far against the door that my cheekbone was nearly crushed.

"Our lives are different now." *Female voice.* "We have our own businesses to run."

"That's another thing I don't understand, Iz." *Iz. Isobel. Shit.* "How can you keep working out of Alexis's office?"

"He's family, Nikos. For all that's happened between the two of us, he's still my family."

Silence. The type of drawn out silence during which a kiss would be entirely appropriate. I turned my head to see if I could peek through the crack in the door.

Wait. What the hell was I doing? How sick was this?

I pulled away from the door and sat on my haunches. "Leave them alone," I said to myself as I got up off the floor.

Just then, the elevator alarm went off. Loud and jangling like a firehouse nightmare. I was done for. Any hotel owner worth his salt would be out here in a flash to see what was going on.

I scrambled back to the elevator and grabbed my shoe. It was stuck between the floor and the edge of the elevator shaft.

"No, no, no," I chanted, grasping the shoe and tugging with all my strength. Finally, the shoe dislodged and sent me hurtling backwards into the elevator wall with a crash.

The white doors unlocked. I grabbed the elevator gate with both hands, heaved it shut, and prodded five or six floor buttons into illumination.

"Close, close, close," I was praying to that sluggish monolith of a metal door to make its way across. But there was no time; the white double doors began to open and I could see a widening sliver of Nikos's bare forearm...

I tossed myself to the back corner of the elevator just as the door rolled shut, hiding me and my one crumpled DKNY pump safely behind it.

"Y'awright, Petal?" Baz called out when I got back to the suite. He and David were nowhere in sight. Blindly, I followed the sound of his voice, barely able to concentrate on anything but the narrowness by which I'd just escaped. James Bond couldn't have done better.

I rounded the corner and passed the bathroom. Then I took a few steps backward and looked in. Baz and David were in the Olympic-sized bath together.

"Where were you?"

"I, uh, went to speak with the owner about your bill. Don't worry about it. Everything's jake."

Both Baz and David had scripts in their hands. David's was quite soggy on the side where he held it.

"What happened to your shoe?" asked David.

I lifted it and gave it a look. Then I rammed the mangled thing onto my foot and hobbled over to the towel rack. I lowered a hand towel onto David's shoulder. "Use it to hold the script," I said limply. "Like Baz is doing."

Baz pointed to his toweled hand. "Good trick, eh? Norah's got loads of them."

"Do you think you boys can handle yourselves without me?" I asked. "I'm just not in the mood for love today."

"Poor Noh-noh," said Baz with a pout. "Why don't you join us in the bubbly? We'll run lines. I know it would just make David's day."

David smiled alluringly, but we both knew it was only for Baz's benefit.

"Very kind, but I'm going to pass."

"Suit yourself. But before you go, would you bring some of that lovely Baklava?"

"Sure thing, B."

"She's too good for me, David," said Baz. "She truly is."

You know, I think he actually meant it.

There's No Place Like Phone

After a long exhausting day of avoiding terminal personal embarrassment, my usual remedy was either Bollywood or a book. Tonight, I sat on my couch and stared at the cold television.

Something still bothered me about Nikos. Wasn't he going to invite me up when I brought him the ice cream? Hadn't he brought me to my apartment and tucked me in when I was unconscious? Didn't he drive me home in the rain? One simply doesn't do these things when one is in love with another woman. Unless one is a real shit, of course. In which case, all bets are off.

My iPhone began to tinkle.

"Norah Pasquale."

"Norah. It's Nikos."

You know that feeling when you slip on a pair of your favorite socks, fresh out of the dryer? That's how my heart felt just then.

"I hope you don't mind my calling. Especially since I got your number from Baz's registration card. Very sneaky of me."

Nikos Santos's voice. On my phone.

I cleared my throat. "Is everything all right? Please don't tell me Baz already trashed his suite. He usually waits until all the other hotels are booked up before he does that. It keeps me on my toes."

Nikos laughed. On my phone.

"Actually, this is more of a personal thing."

I sat down on the floor. He saw me skulking around the penthouse. I wasn't quick enough. Or maybe Isobel, trying to do a little snooping of her own, happened to mention to Nikos that there was this odd little applicant to her clothing website named Norah whom she found out had a very interesting password she thought he'd get a kick out of hearing. Nikos must have put it all together, added it up, and it equaled ripping me a new one for being a creepy stalker. Surely he'd toss Baz out. I'd most certainly get fired.

"I'm calling to ask you to dinner."

I placed my hand over my mouth in order to stop the animal howl that was making its way out of my throat.

"If you're not busy—"

"What about Isobel?" I blurted.

I regretted it the instant I said it. Especially since the question was met with an ominous silence that seemed to go on for eons.

"Isobel." He seemed genuinely confused. "You know her?"

"No, I don't," I half-lied, already mentally struggling to cover my gaffe. "I remember your front desk clerk thinking I was her, and I thought maybe she was...you were—" I wiped the sweat that had formed over my upper lip with the back of my hand.

"Just say yes."

There was a determination in his voice so strong that if he'd asked me to give up all my worldly possessions and live in a Himalayan cave with only a goat as my life-long companion, I would have. Or at least I'd have done some serious travelogue research on the prospect.

"Say yes," he said again, more tenderly. "Let me take you to dinner. I'll answer anything you want to ask."

"Why?"

"Because you'll understand."

"You don't know me."

"I know enough. Now, say yes."

I melted into his sultry baritone. "You win. Yes."

"David's going to flip when he sees this," Helen said, holding a dark gray Armani shirt against her curvy body. We were in Bloomingdale's on her break from the salon. "He's been telling me about this shirt he left back in L.A. that he loves and wears all the time. And I found it! I'm giving it to him tonight."

"Yeah, I'll bet you are," I teased.

"It's our one month anniversary," Helen said somberly. "I want it to be special."

"How's it going?"

"Great," Helen said. She held an indigo silk tie up to the shirt, then put it back down. "But David thinks it's best to lie low. Not go public yet."

"Uh-huh."

"I agree with him, Norah. Look at what's going on: He's about to unleash on millions of viewers a very innovative and vital character who can teach peace and the acceptance of sexual preferences across a whole new sector of society. An openly gay police lieutenant on television is groundbreaking."

"Uh-huh."

"It's better that he doesn't have a lot of personal gossip buzzing around him now. What good would that do for him professionally? It may undermine his entire purpose as a messenger of tolerance."

"Uh-huh. He's gay."

"I *know*," Helen said, crumpling against the display table. She wailed into a stack of neatly folded cashmere sweaters. "Maybe he's just Method. Davey's researching his role."

"Oh, Helen."

"Even if he were, he couldn't be gay-gay. He'd be bi. Obviously."

"Bi-gay or bi-bi? I mean, according to Baz, if a guy is legitimately bi-bi, you're okay. It just means he tastes from the whole buffet of human sexuality. But if he's bi-*gay*, it could mean he's only half out of the closet. My advice? If you find out he's bi-gay, say bye-bye."

Helen leaned against the wall and sighed heavily. "No one has ever made love to me like David does."

"See? That's a good sign. He sounds very bi-bi."

"But *why*?"

"I think it's biological."

"No, why can't I find a bona fide rugged manly man? One who likes only one thing on the buffet."

"Fish?"

"Eww."

"You walked right into that one."

"I'm serious, Norah. How hard is it to find a man like that? Like your Nikos."

I bit my lip. "He's not my anything. He's Isobel's, remember?"

"Oh, honey," sighed Helen, "As long as we're tossing advice around, let me remind you that it is a female's right—no, her obligation—to fight for the man she wants. Nikos is yours. You have to fight for him."

"Wait just a tiny minute. Did you not tell me to stay out of it? That they were in some love-hate obsessive thing? I believe 'Polanski' was used as an adjective."

"Reverse psychology. I had hoped that once the realization sunk in that since you met him you haven't been able to go five minutes without talking about the man—not to mention the fact that every time his name comes up out of context you go all Malaria-like—it would put some fire under your ass to go and make that man your own."

"Wow. I'm a mess, huh?"

"It's amazing how long some people can live with unrequited love burrowing a hole in their intestines."

"Well, don't be too disgusted with me yet."

"Oh?"

"He asked me to have dinner with him tonight."

"Excellent!" Helen jumped up, then cocked her head. "But let me guess. You said, 'Oh, I'd love to N-N-Nikos, but you see, I'm just not in your league. You're probably only asking me out of pity, and while I can certainly understand that—'"

"You can be so cruel," I said to Helen, feigning hurt. "I'm not lame, I'm completely confused. It's better if I don't care one way or another. Cute guy, but he has a wife, so let him go. I think that's admirable, actually."

"Uh-huh," said Helen.

"But the facts are the facts. I embarrass myself at his hotel and what does he do? He doesn't call a cab, he brings me home and *tucks me into my own bed*. Then I bump into him at the gallery and he shows up out of nowhere and drives me home in the rain. Tells me I'm sweet."

"Uh-huh."

"And Isobel! Beautiful as a Parisian sunrise—not that I've ever seen one, but I imagine they're spectacular. She tells me about this man who 'hurt' her. Maybe it *is* Nikos and she's based her life's work on this one man! Can you imagine? How could I not back off?"

"Uh-huh."

"But when Nikos speaks to me it's like warm honey pouring over my whole body. I mean, you don't talk like that to someone unless you want..."

Helen smiled. "To ask her out. Yeah, it's obvious he's not interested." She took David's Armani shirt to the checkout counter. "So, what are you going to do?"

I shrugged. "Have dinner with him. See what happens."

"What is he, a science experiment? You have to know what you want to happen, then *make* it happen."

"Okay. I want him to tie me to the bedpost and torture me with an ostrich feather."

The salesgirl gave me a look, which Helen and I both ignored.

"Be serious, Norah."

"Fine. I want him to come clean about Isobel. If it turns out that they're not married, or seeing each other in some capacity, I want him to invite me back to his penthouse—"

"There you go. Now you're talking."

"—and *then* I want him to tie me to the bedpost and do the feather-torture thing."

"Just keep your goals rooted in your mind and you'll be fine. Stand firm."

"Speaking of standing firm, how are you applying this stellar advice to your own life?"

Helen took her bag from the salesgirl. "Did I mention that the shirt David left in L.A. was in some shade of *violet*?" She huffed a laugh. "Not in my town, honey. Davey's graduating to good old heterosexual New York black. But charcoal's a good start."

I took a detour on my way back uptown, through Central Park, firmly rooting my goals in my mind as I went. Did I really want to spend the rest of my life thinking that every time a man was attracted to me it was some cosmic goof? From now on, no more. I simply had to trust that Nikos genuinely liked me and wanted to spend time with me. And, hell, I was a modern woman; if he was two-timing Isobel, that was his problem, not mine.

I crossed my least favorite part of the park, the precarious stretch of fast-moving skateboarders and rollerbladers in front of the amphitheater. It's a real-life video game where you dodge death while trying to look casual. I was almost all the way across when a kid flipped off his skateboard right into my path. I nearly tripped over him, but stopped short just in time. Fifty bonus points.

"Are you hurt?"

"Nah," said the kid. His knee was scuffed and little beads of blood were already forming on the surface.

"You sure?"

He shrugged, then boarded off again. I watched as he wheeled away, just to be sure, I suppose, that he didn't black out or ram into someone else. That was when I noticed Nikos sitting on a bench by the amphitheater, reading a book. I looked up in the sky to see if God was winking at me; Nikos really was everywhere I went.

I headed right for him to share the funny serendipity, but as I neared the spot where he was sitting, Isobel strode up and stood in front of him, smiling. Nikos closed his book and stood. They embraced a long tender embrace and he kissed her on the cheek, just by her ear. I backed up a few steps and sat on the nearest bench, out of view.

Isobel smoothed the back of her skirt then sat down next to Nikos. She took one of his hands and began to speak. I couldn't hear her from where I was, but I saw her face. Earnest, pained, beseeching. Nikos lowered his head as he listened. He removed his hand from hers and took a deep breath. Whatever he said in response involved shaking his head every now and again.

Isobel looked frustrated. She faced away from him, watching the skaters. Nikos spoke more energetically, took a quick hold of Isobel's arm. She nearly jumped off the bench. He released her, then immediately took her hand back. An apology.

This was no random meeting. The two of them there, and me cowering here reminded me of that scene in *Mujhse Dosti Karoge* where Pooja was the pitiable third leg sulking at the edges of Raj's and Tina's blossoming love.

Who was I kidding? Things were not over between Nikos and Isobel. I had to face facts: Isobel got there first. She had a history with him, one that was much more invested than mine. What place did I have muscling my way in? If Nikos was still with Isobel and still asking me out to dinner, then Nikos was a player, plain and simple. And I just couldn't stomach any more of them.

It was eight o'clock, just around the time I should have been enjoying my almond-encrusted goat cheese appetizer or whatever I would have ordered with Nikos during our dinner date. Instead, I was decked out in my favorite threadbare slip nightgown, feet up on the coffee table and the air conditioner set to Arctic.

I had my favorite comfort combo: Shiraz, a stadium-sized bowl of low-fat, organic popcorn (doused lovingly with melted butter) and, for tonight's viewing pleasure, *Yeh Kya Ho Raha Hai*, Bollywood's answer to *American Pie*. Four college boys learn—with the help of several well-timed dance numbers and snappy songs— that manhood is about loving women, not lusting after them.

A few times I wondered what Nikos was doing, particularly when the handsomely dark bad boy of the film kept finding himself at the center of female attention. But I had these thoughts only for a few vertiginous seconds at a time; I'd never stood anyone up before. I wasn't very good at the no-guilt part.

I must have fallen asleep at some point during the finale. All I know was that I jumped up at the sudden sound of my doorbell and all the kids on the television screen were coupled off and singing gleefully.

Through the peephole, I could barely make out the figure standing there; whoever it was was standing too close to the door. The figure backed up and I caught a glimpse of a few dark curls of hair. Nikos.

I put my head against the door and closed my eyes. What could I possibly say to him? I had planned to call tomorrow and give him some half truth—that Baz had some dietary emergency or something. Lying was not my bag, but I rationalized that if he was going to go out with me behind Isobel's back, it was more than fair play.

But now here he was. And here *I* was standing in my wrinkled slip, quite obviously not tending to Baz, but rather half drunk on Shiraz and Bollywood tunes.

The bell rang again. I jumped. "Yes?" That was all I could manage. I sounded like a perturbed starlet.

"It's Nikos. Can I talk to you?"

Can he talk to me. Good question. He was probably pissed off and with his track record concerning anger and women, albeit his *alleged* track record, it would probably not be at all wise for me to let him into my apartment. I sighed, undid all the bolts, and heaved the door open. Nikos was leaning against the doorframe, hands in his black-linen-trousered pockets, wearing a white cotton shirt and loosened silk tie.

He had probably shaved for our date, but there was already a midnight shadow across his cheeks and chin and the ridge over the top his ruby lips. From the rich smell of heat and outdoors that came from him, I gathered he'd been walking.

Nikos didn't say anything. He didn't even look angry. I opened the door further and headed back to the couch, assuming he'd take the hint to follow me. He did not.

By the time I flipped off the television and sat down, he was still in the doorway, hands still in pockets, still regarding me from the dark sleepiness of his eyes.

"Your mama raised you right," I said. "Come in and sit."

Nikos rolled off his shoulder, stepped in and with one deft motion, shut the door with his heel. Maybe he was pissed off after all. I did a mental check of all the escape routes in my apartment.

"When you didn't show up at the restaurant, I thought you might have had to work at the last minute, so I stopped by Baz's suite," he said, lowering himself into the chair across from me.

I nodded. Lord, he was beautiful.

"Talked to him for an hour. Nice guy. Seems shorter in person."

I nodded again, thankful that for once I had not turned to Baz as my confidant. Not that Baz was the kind of man who would give away secrets; it was that Nikos was the kind of man you find it hard not to give everything to. As it was, I was finding it difficult to stop myself from leaping over the coffee table and straddling him.

"I understand now why you didn't show up for dinner."

"Really."

Nikos reached in his pocket for his cigarettes. "Do you mind?"

"I told you. I like it."

From a drawer in the coffee table, I produced an ashtray Baz had stolen for me from the Rihga.

Nikos smiled at it and lit up. "First of all, I'm very flattered."

"Flattered? What exactly did Baz tell you?"

"He told me you stopped by my place to talk about his bill the other day. And then you left work early. A 'Sad Sally', I think he called you."

I stared at the edge of the coffee table, embarrassed.

"You didn't come by to talk about his bill."

"No, not really."

"But you did come by."

"Yep."

"That was you in the elevator outside the penthouse, wasn't it?"

I nodded. "How did you know?"

"It's standard procedure to review security tapes when an alarm goes off in a hotel."

Shit and double shit.

Nikos thumb-flicked his cigarette into the ashtray. I suddenly felt like we were in an Academy Award film clip.

"One more uncomfortable thing," Nikos said, inhaling. "You lied, didn't you? You know who Isobel is."

"That's three strikes for me. Do you want to show yourself out?"

"You didn't answer the question."

I looked up at him. He must have picked that up from Isobel. Or she from him.

"Yes. I met her once. I'm a member of The Exchange."

"The Exchange?"

"Her website."

"Oh, the clothing business."

"Right." I wasn't going to clarify; it felt bad enough to lie this much to him.

"I told you that at dinner tonight, you could ask me anything you wanted to know," said Nikos. "Do you want to ask me anything now?"

Several questions popped into my head, but only one kept resurfacing. "Do you love Isobel?"

"Yes."

"That's all I need to know," I said, standing.

"Really. That's all?"

"She's a beautiful woman, Nikos. You're both very beautiful. Not that physical beauty is the only reason two people should get together—"

I opened the door for him. Nikos leaned back in the chair and stared at me.

"You suit each other. Darwin would be pleased." I cleared the nervous goo from my throat. "And don't tell me I didn't answer your question. I know."

I was going to have nightmares about this.

Nikos crushed out his cigarette and stood. As he came closer I stood there, grasping for words. "I didn't mean to upset you."

"I'm not upset." Nikos stepped into the hall. "I'm surprised, but not upset."

"Surprised?"

"I didn't peg you for the type to play games."

"What game am I playing?"

"The biggest one of all."

"Oh, really?" My voice shot up an octave and a few decibels. "Well, I think you're the one playing games. Loving someone and going after someone else. And what's with this cryptic stuff? 'The biggest game of all'? What is that?"

Nikos raised his eyebrows. "Amazing. You just went from zero to infuriated in six seconds. I'd look into that, if I were you."

"You know what, Nikos? The last thing I need right now is some man I barely know telling me what to do. Yes, I get angry. Yes, I am vocal about it. So what? It's not like I *hurt* anyone."

"I'd have to disagree," Nikos said. And then he left.

"Is there a book somewhere where I can look this up? Something like, *Top Ten Games Lovers Play*?"

Helen and I were on a field trip with Baz and David to Barnes & Noble in Union Square. Both the celebs were in full disguise, thanks to Helen's handiwork. Nothing too altering, she simply neutralized their spectacularness with off-season sports jackets, baggy chinos, loafers, and ratty baseball caps, all of which she'd picked up at the Goodwill on 23rd Street.

"I'd like to find, *Movie Superstars and the Women Who Love Them*." Helen said, dragging her shimmery, pink-manicured finger along the row of book spines.

We were lingering in the self-help section. Helen had already worked her way through the spines and a few first chapters of all the co-dependency books. Now she was onto the psychology of love.

"Help me out, here," I begged. "What's the biggest game? Playing hard-to-get?"

Helen sighed and slipped a finger between the pages of a book called *Fear & Loving* to mark her place. "Yeah, in 1958 it was."

"I'm serious, Hel."

"You were there. Think. What did you do?"

"Nothing!"

"Well, maybe that's it, then." Helen resumed her reading.

"What? I was supposed to put out? We didn't even have a date. Come on, you know this stuff better than I do."

"Yeah, because I already own half of these books. And you see how well they work for me since I'm happily married."

"But you know more dumb love games than I do."

"True. Okay. Did you tease him?"

"No."

"Lie to him?"

"Yes. But it was only a lie of omission. About The Exchange."

"Good girl. Did you pretend to be someone you weren't?"

"Like who, the Queen of Jordan?"

"Like playing at being a vixen when you're really a prude. Actually, that's tantamount to teasing. And lying." She shrugged. "I'm tapped."

"Wait. Maybe I did lie. After he told me he loved Isobel, he asked if I was sure I didn't want to ask him anything else. I said I was, but part of me wanted to tell him why I cared, how I felt about him. I just didn't see the point. Could that be it, you think?" I grabbed her arm and sent the book flopping to the floor with a papery thud. "Can Nikos read my mind? Do men do that?"

"I don't know, Norah." Helen picked up the book, testily. "And frankly, if he said he loves Isobel, what do you care what he thinks of you?"

She had a point.

From around the corner, in the travel section where we had last left Baz and David, came a chorus of very girly squeals.

Helen closed her book with a snap. "I'll get it," she said, and strode off. Within a few seconds, I heard her quietly negotiating autographs in exchange for privacy. I'd taught her well.

On the shelf was a row of books I hadn't noticed before. *Working Through Anger. Ragebusting. What Your Anger Says About You.*

Nikos, even when you're not here, you're here.

I picked up the last one and leafed through it. Each paragraph had case studies you were supposed to identify with in order to assess your "Anger Type." The back of the book was full of exercises for each Anger Type.

I tucked the book under my arm and headed for the nearest cash register.

The Wounded Warrior

According to *What Your Anger Says About You*, I was a rager who loses control of her calm when she feels she is about to be exposed for a fraud.

> The person who suffers this type of anger commonly possesses low self-esteem. This wounded sense of self is why he fears being deemed a fraud even though he may be nothing of the sort. When this rager is agitated, anger rises like a sword and slashes violently at everything around its host in order to protect from invaders.
> This Anger Type is called **The Wounded Warrior.**

I felt as though I'd been suffering from a disease my whole life that no one had found a name for, never mind a cure, and now there it was in paperback.

I spent the next afternoon and evening doing all the Wounded Warrior journal exercises, meditations, and visualizations the book offered. Whenever I felt tense, I was to light candles or lavender incense, picture myself basking on a Fijian beach. If pangs of self-doubt crept into my mind, I had to slash at them with my mighty warrior sword, replacing self-doubt with images of cradling orphaned children in my arms or freeing enslaved lab animals.

Once I finished discovering all that my anger had to say about me, I went back to the bookstore and bought three more books, one of which actually broke down the physiological stages of anger, complete with multi-colored brain diagrams. I didn't understand the diagrams one whit, but I was convinced I was on the right track.

On the night I finished the last book, I poured a celebratory— and healthily blood-thinning, so I'd learned—glass of Shiraz and settled in to a relaxing evening with Amitabh Bachchan, Bollywood's Sean Connery.

On deck this evening was *Kabhi Khushi Kabhie Gham*. Rough translation: *Sometimes Happiness, Sometimes Tears*. It was the tale of a family torn apart when a son chooses to marry a woman his father disapproves of.

I already knew the ending since Vikram at the rental shop on 28th Street told me. I don't think he meant to. He probably assumed I'd already seen the film since simply *everyone* had. Besides which, I'd already rented most of his inventory.

It didn't matter; there were no real surprises in Bollywood. The Hero either gets The Girl or he gets dead. And in the really good ones, it rains during the finale.

Someone like Vikram could spoil the plot, but unless he also sang all the songs and did all the dance routines, nothing was really ruined at all. In fact, I was very curious to see how familial dysfunction translated into traditional Indian dance.

I fired up the DVD player and turned on the television. To my surprise, Jason was looking back at me. Well, slap me on the back and call me Nancy. Jason Fanking got himself a Comedy Central special.

All alone on the stage except for a stool and a mic stand, Jason paced around in front of a set designed to look like a sports stadium, complete with cutout buxom cheerleaders flanking the wings.

"If the Olympics ever come to New York City," he said, and the crowd let up a whoop. He nodded, waiting for them to settle down. "I'm saying, *if* they do, they ought to put in a few more games that are, let's say, more appropriate to New Yorkers."

The crowd went nuts. They knew what was coming. And so did I. I couldn't help the smile on my face.

"The Two-block Dash. You know, to intercept the traffic cop who's about to ticket your car." Jason high-stepped in place, pumping his arms. "Sidewalk Slalom." Jason mimed weaving between bodies on a crowded sidewalk.

The audience's laughter rose, and just as it began to fall, he spoke with his mouth pressed tight to the mic:

"Sportfucking."

Since this was Comedy Central, what members of the television audience like myself heard was, "Sportf-*beep*-ing."

The howls were tremendous. The camera caught one guy in the audience covering his tear-soaked eyes.

I leaned forward, amazed. He came up with that joke while he was fucking me! I did that!

"Yeah, there's something you see a lot of in the city. Guys on the prowl, looking to do what? *Score.* Come on! Sex is begging to be an official Olympic sport!"

Jason took a sip of water. He was proud of himself. That was evident from his dimpled smirk.

"'Course, my ex-girlfriend wouldn't agree. It took me three tedious dates to convince her that I *really* liked *her* for *her*—blah, blah—before I could *finally* get her into bed. Where's the sport in that?"

A few of the women in the audience booed. He held up a finger. "Now wait a sec, maybe I've stumbled on a new sport, here. Yes: Endurance Bullsh-*beep*-ing."

A few more female boos. I hugged my knees hard to my chest.

"Oh, relax. She didn't even—" A *bleep* sounded over Jason clearly mouthing the word *come*. "Score: Zero."

More laughter. But was it him they were laughing at? Or me? I switched off the television and stared at the blackness for a minute.

I downed the rest of my wine and poured another glass.

I'm his muse, huh? Three tedious dates, huh?

In my gut was that good old familiar throbbing of rage, that swift churning of bile. The more I thought about how that complete misogynist cheating prickwad exposed my insecurities, however anonymously, to the rest of the Comedy Central viewing demographic, the more I wanted to squash his useless single-celled brain into the back of that fake stadium set.

But. I. Remained. Calm.

I closed my eyes, took a deep breath in and exhaled glittering white sparkles of light and happiness that I envisioned wrapping around Jason and transforming him into a little fluffy bunny who hopped froofily away into the forest.

Then I picked up the phone and dialed.

"Nikos. This is Norah. I'm taking you to dinner."

"Well, I—"

"Say yes."

I took Nikos to Desi, an upscale Anglo-Indian restaurant in my neighborhood, just for the double comfort of it. I took the liberty of ordering our entire meal in rudimentary Hindi that I'd practiced for an hour before I left the apartment. Still, it served to impress the crap out of Nikos—not to mention the waiter—which was a good thing. I needed all the self-confidence I could get.

He had barely flipped the white napkin across his tailored lap when I launched in.

"I think I know what my infraction was the other night."

"Infraction."

"'The biggest game on earth' or whatever you called it."

"Ah. And?"

"I lied to you. By omission."

I wasn't going to tell him about The Exchange. Not that lie. Not yet, if ever.

"But before I come clean with what I have to tell you, I need you to clarify something."

"Anything. Name a topic."

"Isobel."

He nodded. "She's my sister."

I sat there, not breathing, letting the words hang in the air while Nikos took a sip of water.

"In-law. She's married to my younger brother Alexis." He squinted. "Are you okay?"

I exhaled, nodded.

"Now, what was it you wanted come clean about?"

"Nothing. I mean, it can wait. Tell me about Isobel."

"Well." Nikos took a warm-up breath. "I was born in Italy and Alexis was born in Greece—my mother was Greek, my father's Italian. Mama owned hotels in both places and two here in New York, so we traveled a lot and lived in them most of the time."

"Sounds exotic."

"It was. And believe it or not, I got used to not having a home. Besides the hotels, of course."

"Of course." In truth, I was trying to imagine a teenaged Nikos with a pocket full of keycards.

"So, I went to school in New York and lived at Hotel Ursula, which was named after my mother. After college, I moved to Paris to get my feet wet in art dealing. I was there about ten years. Then Mama died, leaving the hotels to us kids. Infuriated my father, but then again, almost everything did.

"Lex and Isobel had just gotten married in Greece when Mama died. I invited them to stay with me back in Paris while Lex and I got the New York hotels sorted out. Paperwork, refurbishing, all of that. You with me so far?"

I nodded like an enthralled schoolgirl. "But what about your art dealing?"

Nikos shrugged. "My mother died. I figured I would come to New York and do my art dealing here. I had no idea how much work running a hotel would be. Two hotels, actually, but I'm getting ahead of myself."

"So, Alexis and Isobel are staying with you in Paris."

"Right. One night, after all the business was done, we went out for dinner to celebrate. We got pretty drunk, they went home. I bumped into a friend, so I stayed at the restaurant. About an hour later, Isobel came back, hysterical. She told me that Alexis—"

Nikos stopped. The waiter came over with our wine. There was an uncomfortable polite silence while the wine was poured and tasted and approved. Once the waiter left, I leaned in.

"Alexis what?"

"Hit her." Nikos sighed. "They had a fight. She didn't tell me about what. He backhanded her and then passed out."

"What did you do?"

"Took her home and told her to pack. I brought her with me to New York the next day. She wasn't happy about it, but I wasn't having any of that. Not from him."

"What do you mean?"

155

Nikos shook his head.

"What happened then?"

"I ended up running the conference center for Alexis. He's probably still living in my Paris flat. I haven't heard from him since we left. That's because he knows," Nikos bristled, "how serious this is." His face clouded over with a sudden fierceness I had never seen in him.

"How serious is it, exactly? Besides the fact that it was an awful thing to do."

"Our father used to beat us," he said. "All of us. My mother, too. I swear she got cancer because she stressed herself to death. When we were little boys, Alexis and I made a pact that we would never—"

I reached over and put my hand over Nikos's; it had been clutching the side of the table in a death grip. He relaxed and put his large, warm hand over mine.

"I do love Isobel. I feel very protective of her. But there's nothing romantic going on between us."

"Are you sure?"

"I just told you."

"I mean, are you sure *she* knows there's nothing going on?"

Nikos took his hand away. "What are you saying?"

I had just pirouetted into a minefield. "She must feel very indebted to you," I said carefully.

"It's not as though she hasn't helped me. My god," he laughed. "You should have seen me back in Paris. I was a mess. I drank too much, slept around. I wore the same grubby chinos and workshirt every day. Ratty canvas sneakers with a hole in one toe. The only suit I owned was the one I wore to my mother's funeral."

Imagining him so undone made me smile.

"My hair was down to the middle of my back—"

A little moan escaped from deep in my throat, but thankfully Nikos didn't seem to hear.

"When we came to the States, Isobel bought me a whole new wardrobe, cleaned me up. She said I'd be taken more seriously in my business. She was right."

"She did a very spiffy job."

"I loathed it. It was exactly how Alexis dressed. He inherited Mama's classiness. But I guess I've gotten used to the spiffiness, as you call it."

"So, what happened to the infamous chinos?"

"To this day, I have no idea what Iz did with them. Sometimes I miss the shit out of them." Nikos regarded me a moment and cocked his head. "What?"

"Have you been listening to yourself? You essentially save Isobel's life by whisking her off to New York, a place where she most likely doesn't know anyone but you. Then she dresses you up like her *husband*?" Nikos stared at the bread basket. "Don't you think there's any possibility that, over all this time, Isobel may have developed feelings for you?"

Nikos leaned back in his chair. "Do you know something I don't?"

I couldn't lie. Not again. But I couldn't tell the full truth, either.

"I don't know anything. I don't know her," I sighed. "Let's just say it's not unreasonable to believe that Isobel loves you *differently* than you love her. Or if not," I took a sip of wine, hoping it would bolster me, "she may not want anyone else to love you."

"That's ridiculous."

"It's not my business; I'm not your family. I think you need to work it out. All three of you."

The food came, then, with all its spicy colors and fiery aromas, but we were somehow immune to their magic now. Nikos and I ate in silence.

He didn't put up too much fuss when I offered to pay the bill, for which I was grateful. I let him drive me home. Strangely, there was one free parking spot on the entire street, and it was right in front of my door.

"I'll take that as a sign," said Nikos.

We sat on my couch with glasses of my remnant Shiraz, listening to whatever I already had in the CD player, which happened to be an Erik Satie compilation. I lit a candle on the coffee table, but as it happened, I wasn't sure I was feeling all that romantic. The evening's conversation had left me in a sort of emotional limbo. I actually found myself feeling sorry for Isobel.

Maybe she and Nikos were meant to be together. She'd been through hell. He saved her. He loved her. After all the Bollywood romances I'd seen, I knew better than to be a fallen log on the well-worn path of true love. Cheesy as they might seem to the untrained heart, those films taught me that love is Divine, stemmed from a universal power we cannot control.

The silence between Nikos and me was transcendent. I was curled up on my usual solitary dent in the couch, listening to both the lilting piano of Gymnopédie No. 3 and Nikos's measured breathing next to me. He stared at the candlelight. For a while, so did I, trying to imagine what Nikos was seeing, what he might be thinking. After a few minutes I almost forgot he was there, but then I looked over. And there he was.

Nikos took in a slow breath through his nose and shifted. When he spoke, his voice was gentle and low, as if he'd just woken from sleep.

"It's late. I need to get back."

I nodded and began to lift myself off the couch. Just as I did, Nikos slid over, took my face in his hands and kissed me. Softly and long. It took me only a moment to find his rhythm, match it. There was something we both knew, this miraculously identical *something*, and were speaking it silently, right into each other's mouths.

When it was over, I managed to show him to the door. Nikos stepped into the hallway, but turned back toward me.

"Earlier tonight, you said you had something to tell me. Tell me now."

I smiled at him. "I just did."

Handsome, Hair, and Hanuman

"Have you seen today's paper?" Baz was in the makeup trailer, having just had his face put on. Gina currently had the tender tips of a brush to David's lower eyelids. Today was David's first day of shooting. He was cramming; dog-eared pages of the script lay in his lap. In Baz's hands was the latest issue of *Star Secrets*.

"Who are you sleeping with now, Baz?" I asked, cheerily.

"You," said David, looking up from his script. "Imagine that."

"Don't move," Gina admonished, "unless you want eyes like Cleopatra."

Baz held up the newspaper. "Newspaper" was not the correct term for this publication. "Rag" would be closer. "Inky toilet paper" would be right on the money.

On the front page of the entertainment section was the weekly column, "Gabby's Gab," the latest celebrity gossip from notoriously nosey New Yorker, Gabrielle Rosenblatt.

Brit Babe Baz's Secretary To Become Mrs. Smithy?
Oh, Captain, my captain! Could it be true? Get your panties in a twist boys (and girls, apparently), because Gabby's gotten word that British *Handsome Blue* star

> Baz Vancouver has proposed to his secretary of six years, 34-year-old Norah Pasquale....

I tossed the paper on the makeup table. "I can't read this. It's just so *wrong*."

"Technically it isn't," said Baz. "I did propose."

"'*Secretary*'? Gabby can kiss my ass with 'secretary'."

"Don't worry, Petal. I'm going to tell them you're pregnant and I'm only doing the honorable thing."

"How chivalrous." I smacked my forehead. "My god, how many people are going to see this?"

"Only the intellectually starved general populous and—"

"And everyone at the hotel," David chimed in.

"Don't *move*, damn it," said Gina.

I squeaked. "The hotel?"

"Oh, yes," Baz said with a chuckle. "Apparently they have to *give* these dreadful things away. I saw a stack of them in the lobby."

"I have to go," I said, grabbing the paper and stuffing it into my bag.

"You just got here. Stay. It's Davey's coming out party. Today he tells the lads-in-blue he's in love with me."

"I'll be back, I promise."

"Don't be so upset, Norah," said Baz. "Why can't you take it in stride? The way Helen did that night?"

David jolted. "What about Helen?"

Gina tossed her brush at the mirror. It struck the reflection of David's right eye.

"Ouch. That looked like it hurt," said David. Gina huffed off, mumbling about coming back when she could do her work without interruptions. "So, what's this about Helen?"

"She saved my arse a couple of months ago," said Baz, "after a very unfortunate incident with a very psychotic boy. It was delicious; Helen and I left Norah's building together in a perfectly scandalous way. Started the whole 'Is Baz Bi?' phenomenon. The viewer poll was up on the *Entertainment Tonight* website for six weeks."

"*Are* you bi?" There was a ripple of jealousy in David's voice.

"No, love. I am ambisexual. We discussed this. The other night? When I was making sweet love to you?"

"Very funny, Baz-hole," said David.

"Okay, boys. I'm out." I said, kissing Baz's cheek.

"I'll have to re-powder now."

"Cheerio!"

"Listen, if you're leaving to do damage control at the hotel, I can assure you it's pointless. Tourists love freebies. I'll bet there isn't one copy left in that lobby."

"If there is one and I can destroy it, I will be a happy woman."

Baz eyed me. "I'd take that personally if I didn't have a gut feeling you're really off to see your scrumptious Mr. Santos."

I put my bag down. "What makes you say that?"

"Oh, puh-lease." Baz began powdering the spot on his cheek where I'd kissed him. "You think I haven't noticed? The way you've been acting all scatterbrained, twittering about every time we've been in the hotel, looking over your shoulder for him like some knobby-kneed schoolgirl?" He put his fingers to his mouth and feigned a teenaged crush. "'*Oo! Is he here? Will I see him? What'll I say? My hair's a mess.*'"

"Wrong. My hair is always fabulous."

Baz smirked. "Why, just last night—the same night you mysteriously requested to leave your cell phone off, I might add—I happened to bump into one Nikos Santos at the hotel bar."

"You did?" I did my utmost to feign non-chalance.

"I did. He said he was on his way out to have dinner with you."

"He did?"

"He did. I also happened to be at the bar when he returned. Don't look at me like that, either of you. I was being a good boy. Anyway, this time Nikos didn't notice me. That's because he was singing to himself."

"He was?" I was beaming involuntarily.

"He was."

"What was he singing?"

Baz looked at David and then back at me. "What is this, *Name That Tune*? I don't know. A nice little song. All lovey and birdies flying round, all right?"

"Right. Sorry. Still, I should go."

"So, go. I shall try to get over the anguish I feel that you didn't tell me you were in love."

"Baz. *Shush*. I don't know what this is, okay?"

"You are so hard in love," David said. "Helen says so all the time."

Baz looked over at him. David, finally exposed, opened his mouth and shut it again.

"Not you, too," said Baz. "Oh, Christ. I'm going to die an old maid."

"Look, I just don't want to jinx this thing with Nikos," I said.

Baz smiled warmly. "You can't. If it's meant to be, it's not yours to jinx."

"Do you watch Bollywood, too?"

"Are you drunk?"

"If only. Wish me luck."

"Luck," Baz and David said simultaneously.

"Jinx!" said Baz. "Not you, Petal. That was for David."

Baz was wrong; there was exactly one copy of the incriminating inky toilet paper left on a table in the lobby of the

Hotel Ursula. However, the entire entertainment section had been mysteriously ripped out. I snatched it up anyway and shoved it into my bag.

At the far end of the lobby, though, I saw a complete stack, still bound in string.

Jackpot.

I went over to the stack and lifted it, but it was heavier than I thought. My knees nearly gave out. As I bent down to give the bundle another heave, a voice spoke from behind me.

"Norah. Nice to see you again."

I dropped the stack with a thud and turned. Claire. She was sitting in a plush chair, reading a paperback.

"I didn't know you had a paper route on the side," she said snidely. "A little extra cash never hurts, huh?"

I suppose she thought she was being witty, but I was rubbed entirely the wrong way. That was due in part to the fact that I knew perfectly well that where there was Claire, there was Isobel. And this time I knew exactly where "there" was.

"I'm recycling," I said. "Doing my bit for the city, you know. No one ever reads this trash anyway."

"Oh, I do," said Claire cattily. She held up the ripped out article. "I guess congratulations are in order. Have you and the Captain set a date?"

"Sure, sure. We'll send you and Isobel an invite," I said, as lightly as possible, but my temper was rising. I knew if I continued this conversation, Claire was going down for the count. With a smile plastered to my face, I turned toward the front desk.

"Are you here to see Isobel?" Claire asked. "You know, she's just upstairs if you want to wait."

"Now, why would I come *here* to see Isobel?"

Claire smiled at me knowingly. Something very bad was going on.

"Excuse me." I kicked the stack of papers to the front desk and tapped the bell. Up popped a female clerk from behind the counter. It was the same woman from the night I'd checked Baz in. I nearly screamed.

"Oh! Hi!" I said, loud enough for Claire to hear. I wanted to be sure she got the message that I came here. A lot. "I haven't seen you around."

"I was here. I just dropped my pen," said the stoic clerk, holding up her pen as proof.

"No, I meant—never mind. Would you please just give a quick ring to Nikos and tell him *Norah* is here to see him?"

I shot a defiant look at Claire as the clerk picked up the Big Red Phone. Claire remained icy, but I was unfazed. Now she'd see some real preferential treatment.

The clerk hung up the phone. "Mr. Santos said he'll speak with you later."

Claire's smug grin burned a hole into my back.

"Right. Well. That's actually better for me. I have to get back to work anyway. I'll just be taking these off your hands." I lifted the bundle and pulled it up into my arms as casually as I could without giving myself a hernia.

The clerk was too stunned to object.

"Give Isobel my best," I chirped over my shoulder, en route to the front door.

"Tell her yourself," said Claire.

Sure enough, just as I swiveled my head around, Isobel stepped out of the elevator. Her hair, I noticed immediately, was uncharacteristically disrupted.

Isobel must have been as shocked to see me as I was her because she froze in mid-step, her fingers still in the process of smoothing back her trademark and currently off-kilter chignon.

"Why, Norah," said Isobel, a little breathless. "What brings you to the Hotel Ursula?"

"Recycling," said Claire from the lobby.

Isobel gave the once-over to my bundle of newspapers and smirked. I hated Claire.

"Business," I said. "My boss stays here, remember?"

"Don't you mean your fiancé?" Claire called out.

"Can't you curb your help, Isobel?" I said hotly over my shoulder. "A good assistant should know her place."

"Norah?" The desk clerk cut in, hanging up the Big Red Phone. "Mr. Santos says he's free now. You can go right up."

I imagine that when the world does finally come to an end and there are people running through the streets screaming in terror, molten lava flowing down Fifth Avenue, and there's looting, killing, and general dread spanning the globe, it won't be nearly as horrifying as the look Isobel was giving me at that very moment.

To cover myself, I could have bluffed something about seeing to Baz's room service tab or something. But Isobel wasn't stupid. Nikos would never invite a guest's personal assistant up to his penthouse to do business. Besides, there was something about seeing Isobel and her messy hair that flipped a switch in me.

"No worries," I said the clerk. "Tell him I'll see him later." Then I leaned close to Isobel so only she could hear me. "I think we'd better let the poor boy rest, don't you?"

Isobel snuffed up a tight breath. I stepped back and adjusted my bundle. "Bye, Claire!" I yelled, but I kept my eyes on Isobel.

It wasn't until I was in the cab and could no longer see the Hotel Ursula from my window that I burst into tears. How, after our wonderful night together? After the confessions, the silence, that *kiss*. How could he go and mess up Isobel's hair like that? My god! I curled up on the seat and sobbed right into the stack of newspapers. I didn't even care if the cabbie heard me.

I rolled my head to the side so I could read the license attached to the back of his seat.

"Bhuvan Krishnamurthy," I sniffled. Then, with a breathy sigh, I said the cab driver's name again, pretending to be a Hindi film heroine.

"Yes, Miss," said Bhuvan.

I wiped my nose with the back of my hand and sat up. From what little I could see in the rear view, Bhuvan Krishnamurthy was a youngish Indian man with smiling brown eyes.

"Your pronunciation is very good, Miss."

"*Dhanya-waadh*," I thanked him in Hindi.

Bhuvan Krishnamurthy laughed. He told me that *dhanya-waadh* was very formal and really only used to thank someone for a huge favor. "Like saving your child from drowning in the River Ganga."

"Close enough," I muttered.

On his dash was a tiny framed picture of a Hindu god: Half man, half monkey.

"The god of loyalty," I said, the heat rising to my face again.

"You know Hanuman," said Bhuvan, cheerily.

"Yeah," I said, and leaned back in my seat. "But what's Hanuman done for me lately?"

170

"No need to question. *Ishwar aik hai.* The gods are always with us."

"I know."

"Then why you are crying, may I ask you?"

"I am crying, Bhuvan Krishnamurthy, because I love a man who doesn't love me."

"I should think that fighting for your *sanam*, your beloved, will make you strong."

"Oh, I'm not fighting. I swore off that whole anger thing."

"You are at peace, then."

I looked into the rear view mirror. Bhuvan looked back at me. His dark eyes awaited my response. They were no longer smiling.

The Wounded Warrior Writes A Letter

It was nearly one in the morning when the *Handsome Blue* shoot at Bryant Park finally ended. Four scenes, fifteen hours. After she got off work, Helen sat with me on the sidelines as David's personal cheerleader.

Every time he finished a take, she had his Evian waiting and Gina somewhere nearby to touch up his face. It was adorable. And honestly, I was relieved to have her there to take some of the pressure off.

"Here's what you should do," she said as we cruised the leftovers at the craft service table. Helen had filled her plate with the least offensive offering: raw baby carrots and baked potato chips. "You ought to go onto our little website and post something about Nikos. Something really nice."

"Are you nuts? Isobel knows my username. She'll know it was me."

"So what? Were you or were you not kissed by this man?"

"I was more than kissed. I was mind-melded."

"Then that is a perfectly good reason to tell the truth about him."

"And when she finds out?"

"What's the worst that could happen?"

I took those words with me as I sat at my computer that night. This was the first time I'd entered anything into The Exchange as a full-fledged member. Figures my first contribution would be a bombshell.

I typed in "Nikos Santos," and stared at the red flag for a while before clicking on his name. A new field appeared on the screen, ready for me to fill with anything I had to say.

But I didn't want to share my experience with Nikos. I wanted only to remove that terrible stigma Isobel had attached to him.

I began typing:

Dear Fellow Ex-changers:

I am aware that Nikos Santos is a Red-flagged Man. I am writing today not to reveal my dating experience with Nikos Santos, but to humbly request the removal of this Red Flag status from his name. I know one thing: Nikos Santos is not violent. In fact, his life has been spent avenging violent behavior, particularly against women.

Whether he possesses any other trait that might have caused him to be red-flagged, such as being unfaithful, I do not know. However, I have recently come to the conclusion that only with open communication can we women discover the truth about the men we date. Anything else is a lie.

Respectfully,
BOLLYWOMAN

That was that. I hit return and then I hit the sack.

Helen and I went down to Gilda's for brunch the next afternoon.

"I saw your posting this morning."

"Yeah? What do you think?"

"I'm all for it. You're so cool. Will you be my best friend?"

"Can't. I already am." I took a sip of my mimosa. "I just hope Isobel takes it well."

"She won't," said Helen. "But screw her." Helen took a pause. "Now let's play 'good news, bad news'."

"Uh-oh. Good news first."

"I think David is going to propose."

I picked a stray piece of orange pulp from my lip. "To whom?"

"Don't be a wiseass."

"This is the same David who doesn't want to go public with the fact that he's dating you? Think, woman."

"Do you pick up a paper, ever?"

She reached over and removed from her bag a copy of *The New York Times* Arts & Leisure section. A side bar featured a very handsome photo of David and Helen dining at Le Cirque. Its caption referred to Helen as David Astor's "lithe and lovely girlfriend."

"Oh, sure. You get classy press in *The Times*, I get trashy lies in gossip rags. How did David take it?"

"He's the one who introduced me to the reporter as his girlfriend. Man, we had the best sex that night."

"Congrats." In the process of handing the paper back to her, another photo caught my eye. "Hang on a second."

It was a small picture of Nikos and Isobel. Nikos wore a tux, and Isobel, a white gown. They had their arms around each other. A diamond ring sparkled on her finger.

Above the photo was the headline, SANTOS HOTEL MAGNATES TO HOLD FAMILY GALA. Underneath, it read: *Santos wedding in Paris: Nikos and Isobel Santos.*

My hand shook as I turned the paper around toward Helen. "Did you see this?"

Helen bit her lip. "That was the bad news. I didn't know if you'd seen it. Guess not, huh?"

"No," I said, the mimosa doing somersaults up into my throat.

"She's pretty," said Helen, wincing.

I glowered at her.

Helen poked at the article. "It says they're holding the bash at Hotel Ursula and closing the place to *all guests* that weekend."

"I wonder when Nikos was going to tell me about the party. Or about Isobel marrying her way through the Santos clan," I slumped in my seat.

"Well," said Helen, regarding the photo again, "That's obviously an old picture. Look at the gown. Very past-season. If he did marry her, they're through now."

I wrapped one arm around my souring stomach. "God, maybe Nikos wasn't *going* to tell me he and Isobel were married."

Helen rolled her eyes. "You and your soap operatic paranoia. It's a wonder you can leave the house. Here's an idea, Norah: *Ask him.*"

I put my hand over the picture. "Can I keep this?"

"Of course. But can I have my photo back?"

I ripped out the Nikos article and handed the whole section to her. Our food arrived and, much to my surprise, I was ravenous.

"What do we do about this party thing?" asked Helen, dropping a bump of butter onto her Challah French Toast.

"Now? Nothing. Let's eat. I'm probably just going to end up stress-puking later anyway."

I sliced the edge of my fork into my spinach and feta omelet. Helen made a tiny noise deep in her throat. I thought for a second that she was choking. When I looked up, I saw she was indeed choking, but it wasn't the life-threatening kind.

I followed her gaze over my shoulder. Isobel was heading straight for our table. She wore an ivory pantsuit with a silk Hermès scarf tied at her neck. I was in track pants and the Smurfette T-shirt I'd slept in.

"It's Sunday, for god's sakes. Doesn't this woman ever give the *haute couture* thing a rest?"

"What do you want? She's French." Helen was staring, entranced. "Man alive, she's even more gorgeous in person."

I put my fork down. "Perhaps I'll just throw up now instead," I said.

"No way, cupcake," said Helen, snapping out of it. "Be strong. Don't take any shit."

"Take no shit. Got it."

"But don't get angry. Rise above her."

"Wounded Warrior power. Right."

"And *breathe.*"

I took a breath and exhaled it as Isobel descended upon our table.

"Isobel, this is Helen. Helen, Isobel," I said in not much more than a monotone.

Helen half-stood and put her hand out, but Isobel never even looked at her. Her eyes were glued on me.

"That stunt you pulled is not acceptable."

"Which one? The web posting? Or dating Nikos?"

Isobel pounded her fist on the table, making the silverware jump. Helen grabbed her mimosa flute to stop it from toppling.

"You have no idea what it means to be a Santos, Norah. None. You do not know us, and you never will. Consider your membership to The Exchange revoked." She straightened and looked down her perfect nose at me. "One more thing: Stay away from Nikos. I am warning you just this once."

I calmly took the napkin out of my lap and dropped it on the table. I stood up and faced Isobel, eye-to-Hermès scarf.

"Norah," Helen said, cautiously.

"It's all right, Hel," I said, my eyes locked on Isobel's. "Despite your history with Nikos, Isobel—most of which I don't know, that's true—Nikos is his own person. Who he decides to be with is his choice, not yours. Now. You've interrupted my meal and been rude to my friend, so I'm going to ask you—just this once—to leave."

Isobel turned in a huff, but I grabbed her wrist. "One more thing: Don't ever threaten me again. I don't respond well to threats. Things tend to get broken. Like promises, silences. That sort of thing. Get my drift?"

I released her, sat back down, and replaced the napkin on my lap. I looked back up at Isobel, who stood frozen in place. "Was there something else?"

"I feel sorry for you," she said. "I really do."

"Likewise."

Isobel turned and strode away, leaving a softly lingering trail of Coco Chanel that nearly gagged me.

"My god," Helen said. "I think I just peed. You are one scary motherfucker."

I hacked off a piece of omelet and stared at it on my fork. "Yep. I'm going to barf."

"Stop it. You're my hero."

"No."

"But you weren't serious about that broken secret thing were you?" She leaned over and whispered. "You're not going to expose The Exchange."

"If I have to, I will. What do you care? You don't need it anymore, Mrs. Astor."

Helen perked up. "Will you be my Best Woman?"

"Sure, if I don't get bumped off by the French Fashion Mafia first."

Back at the apartment, Helen and I arrived to find two dozen roses at my door. They were in a long white box, with the cover delicately slid off to the side to expose them.

"Holy sheep dip," said Helen. "Who are they from?"

"If they're not from who I think they're from, I'm going to have to jump out my window."

I bent down to slide the card off the box just as Mrs. Garibaldi opened her door. The smell of frying peppers and garlic wafted into the hallway.

"*Ciao, ragazze!*" Mrs. Garibaldi wiped her hands on her apron. "Very tall man here for you, Norah. I see through door hole." Mrs. Garibaldi winked. "He is Italian, no?"

I looked at Helen. She put her hands over her mouth to stop from laughing.

"I guess I can cross suicide off my list of things to do today," I said, taking the card out of its envelope. "'Dearest Norah,'" I read loudly enough for deaf Mrs. G. to hear, "'Sorry I missed you, but I was missing you. Nikos.'"

"Oh," cried Helen. "Good puppy!"

"Nikos?" said Mrs. Garibaldi, disappointed. "*Questo non è un nome italiano.*"

"His last name is Santos. His mother was Greek."

"Eh," said Mrs. Garibaldi with a shrug. "*Mezzo-italiano.* 'S'okay."

"That's okay with you, Mrs. G?"

"Greeks have bad temper."

"Not like Italians," huffed Helen.

"Don't start, she's an old woman," I whispered so Mrs. Garibaldi wouldn't hear.

Mrs. Garibaldi waved a dismissive hand in the air and went back inside.

"Big bad ol' Isobel would die if she saw this," said Helen.

"Do me a favor," I said, as we unlocked our doors. "Don't even say her name. I don't think my digestive system can take it."

"Oh, hey. When you call Nikos—which I know you'll do immediately upon shutting that door—find out what he's planning to do with David and Baz during the hotel bash. It's in two weeks already."

"Sadly, I have more than that to find out."

Helen gave me a sympathetic pout then blew me a kiss for strength.

I didn't call Nikos immediately. I was still stinging from the Isobel encounter. I took the article from my purse and smoothed it out on the coffee table. It was painful to look at the two of them so happy together, but I made myself. I had to be ready for whatever explanation Nikos would give me.

There was only one way to get that explanation. I dialed the hotel and was immediately patched through.

"I got the flowers," I told Nikos. "That was the sweetest thing anyone's ever done for me."

Nikos laughed. "Then you've been sorely deprived. I'll do my best to make up for lost sweetness."

I leaned back on the couch in blissful delirium. Article? What article? No. Must focus. I had to be strong. Push forward. I needed answers.

"Listen, Nikos, I have to talk to you about something. A couple of things, actually."

"Tell me when I get there."

"You're coming over? Now?"

"Well, we should hit the road before the traffic gets bad."

"Again with the cryptic talk. What's going on?"

"I'm kidnapping you. We're going Upstate to Daag's place for the night. He did really well with his show and he wants to have us over to celebrate."

"He said that? He wants *us* over?"

"Sure. He knows all about you."

Daag knows all about me. And why? It must be because Nikos told him all about me. Oh, joy of joys!

"But what about work? Baz will need—"

"I already spoke with Baz. You're free. Now go pack."

"Yessir, Sir."

"See you in fifteen."

I bolted out the door and banged on Helen's. "Helen, open up. *Helen!*"

She opened her door, wrapped in a towel.

"You okay? I was just getting in the shower."

I grabbed her shoulders and jumped up and down. "We're an 'us'! Nikos called us an 'us'! And Daag knows all about me!"

Helen hugged me hard. "Oh, honey! I have no idea who Daag is, but that is su-fucking-*perb*."

"Daag? The Dutch artist guy? From the Robin date."

"Daag! The Dutch artist guy who now knows about you! Hooray!"

We jumped around jubilantly. Helen's towel dropped to her feet. Which was precisely when Mrs. Garibaldi poked her head out of her door again.

She took one look at me clinging to the very naked Helen and shook her head. When she closed her door, we heard all three locks click.

I stopped jumping.

"What is it?" Helen scooped her towel back up and wrapped it around herself. "Oh, don't worry about Mrs. G. She probably forgot already."

"Not that," I said. "Nikos is on his way over to pick me up for a trip Upstate."

"Great!"

"Overnight, Helen."

"Even better."

"Well, technically, this will be date number three."

"Oh, honey, if you made it to 'us', you're way beyond the 'rules of dating' crap."

"But I haven't slept with him yet."

"Looks like you'll be getting some fine *mezzo*-Italian booty now, babe. Have a blast. I'm going in. It's freezing."

I grabbed her arm. "He's so perfect and passionate, Helen. He makes me want to eat everything with my fingers."

"That's a positive thing, Norah."

"But it's been so long. I'm out of practice. What if I'm no good? What if—"

"I'm not listening to this. You are a total sex goddess. Remember that."

"I'm a Wounded Warrior."

"A Wounded Warrior-slash-Sex Goddess. Now let me shower." I let go of her arm. "Don't forget to pack condoms."

I moaned. "I hate condoms."

"We all do, honey, but that's life. You can thank a little African monkey for that. Have a nice time."

On the drive up to Hudson I learned Daag owned not one home, but two, the latter of which was where we would be staying. I had a brand new box of extra thin, Nonoxinol-9-slathered LifeStyles, but hadn't packed much in the way of clothing. Somehow I assumed we'd be tromping through muddy back yards or writhing around naked for most of the time.

Although I was having trouble concentrating on anything but our inevitable first sexual encounter (Would we attack each other as soon as we got in the door? Would it be later that night, in front of the fireplace, after a bottle of wine? Or would we flirt around until our last hours before returning then go at it like a couple of hormone cases?), I had managed to tell Nikos that I'd seen the article about the Santos family hotel gala.

"I was meaning to tell you about that. Don't worry about a thing. We're refusing reservations that weekend, but Baz and David are welcome to stay. In fact, I hope you'll come to the party."

"That's a relief. I mean about their rooms. I'll tell them."

"Something else on your mind?"

"Yeah, actually. The picture. The one that went along with the article."

"What about it?"

I huffed a laugh. "I don't know. I thought you might want to mention your wedding photo to me."

Nikos moaned. "You are something else. Poor baby."

He squeezed my leg. Fire shot straight through to my groin. This man was dangerous.

"Did you look closely at the picture?"

I took it out of my purse and unfolded it. Nikos gave me a funny look, probably because I was carrying it with me.

"It was taken at Isobel's and Alexis's wedding," Nikos said. "They cropped him out for some reason. That," he said, pointing to another hand on Isobel's waist, "is Alexis."

I hadn't seen the hand before, but now I saw that it had a wedding band on its ring finger.

"Handsome, isn't he?" Nikos said.

"What a dumbass. I'm sorry."

"It's all right. I can see why you'd be confused."

I leaned over and kissed Nikos's sideburn. He smelled so delicious that I considered jumping him right there in the driver's seat.

"Nikos, I am going to make a concerted effort to enjoy this. To enjoy *us*."

"Good," said Nikos, his eyes on the road.

"Right after I say this one last thing."

He flipped his eyes skyward for a second. "Okay, shoot."

"Isobel came by today. She doesn't want me to see you. She told me that; she said it flat out. Threatened me, actually."

Without a word, Nikos pulled over onto the side of the highway and put the car in park. It shook with every whizzing vehicle that went past us. He looked hard at me.

"I swear I'm not lying, Nikos. I'm not even exaggerating. I wasn't going to tell you at all, but I don't want any secrets."

"What did she say, exactly?"

"She said I don't understand what it means to be a Santos, and that I never will."

Nikos cracked his window and lit a Marlboro.

"And she said she would only warn me once," I braced myself. "To stay away from you."

Nikos closed his eyes. The muscles of his jaw rippled a few times.

I clenched my fists and unclenched them. "There's something else. When I stopped by the hotel the other day, I bumped into Isobel when she came down from your penthouse." He looked at me. I could barely breathe. "Her hair—"

"Oh, *Christ*," There was a sudden intensity in Nikos that took me completely off guard, almost frightened me. "Yes, Norah. Yes. Okay?"

"No, not okay. I don't know what you're saying." My hands had begun to shake. I balled them into fists and wedged them under my legs.

"I asked Isobel if she was in love with me. I didn't say anything about you; I made it sound like I'd figured it out myself."

"What happened?"

Nikos crushed out his cigarette and exhaled. The smoke hit the steering wheel and split into two willowy streams. He spoke softly. "She kissed me."

The leather squeaked underneath me as I turned back around in my seat and faced the open road. I sat harder on my fists to stop myself from repeatedly pommeling the car door, which I wanted to do so badly that my body ached. Five or six more cars whizzed past before Nikos spoke again.

"I didn't let it go on."

"But you let it happen," I said evenly.

"You don't understand."

"So everyone keeps reminding me. I'm thinking maybe this trip isn't such a good idea."

"Norah, now goddamn it—"

"Don't you dare," I said, turning on him. "It's not my fault I don't understand what's gone on in your family. It wasn't my decision to be kept in the dark. You have two choices, Nikos. Either turn this car around and take me home or *make* me understand."

When we pulled into the long gravel drive, Daag was waiting for us in the garden. He had a handful of fresh basil, which he lifted in greeting. The house was large and white with what looked to be at least fifty acres of field and woods surrounding it.

"This is the guest house?" I asked as we got our luggage from the trunk.

"That's what Daag calls it. Wait until you see his place."

I slung my bag over my shoulder and headed up the drive. Nikos slammed the trunk closed.

"Norah, wait." I turned around to face him. "We'll talk tonight. I promise you won't be in the dark anymore." He bent down and kissed me gently on the lips.

"There's time for that later, you two." Daag made his way up the drive, his workboots crunching on the gravel. He took my bag from me and led us into the house.

If I'd ever had a fantasy as a kid about the perfect country home, this would have been it. Rustic, but modern. Spacious, yet full of homey knick-knacks. There was, as I'd imagined there would be, a monumental brick fireplace in the living room. Braided rugs everywhere. Shaker furniture. Big wooden slab of a dining room table.

The kitchen was bigger than my entire living room. I imagined myself standing barefoot in it, baking wholegrain bread from scratch, while listening to NPR. Then I looked over at Nikos and nearly crumpled from the magnitude of so much beauty in such close proximity.

Daag led us up the spiral wooden stairs to the bedroom. I was ahead of Nikos, following Daag. Halfway up, I looked behind me and caught Nikos regarding my behind, so I swung my hips at him for a few steps until he pinched me and I let out a yelp.

"I'm glad there's a hundred fifty yards between the houses," Daag said. "I think it will be noisy here tonight."

My jaw dropped in mock-offense and Nikos winked at me.

I was a happy, happy woman. Even happier when I saw the bedroom. The king-sized mahogany four-poster bed was enough to send me into ecstatic arrest. But at the foot of the bed, against the wall, was another fireplace, this one made of stone, and a white flokati rug in front of it.

"Jesus Christmas," I said under my breath.

"The rug's from Greece," Nikos said, having noticed me gawking at it. "It was my mother's."

"You like the house?" asked Daag.

I slid my shoes off, hopped up on the bed and bounced a couple of times. "No, I think it's disgusting. I hate it here."

Daag looked at Nikos, slightly alarmed.

"Sarcasm," Nikos said with a smirk. "The cornerstone of American humor."

Daag clapped his hands together and let out a laugh. "Good! We worked so hard on this place."

"We?" I asked.

"Yes," said Daag, proudly. "Nikos and I made almost everything in this house."

"Renovated," Nikos corrected, dropping his bag on a cedar chest by the door.

"Furniture, too," said Daag. "Like this bed."

I got up on my knees, and grabbed hold of one of the wooden posts. "You did this? I can't believe it. It's so...*big*."

"I'm going to have to ask you to stop stroking that post, Miss," said Nikos. Daag laughed again and said something about heading over to his house for drinks.

At that moment, I wanted Nikos so much that I was sure if I made a motion to get off the bed I would orgasm right there in front of them both. I did let go of the post, though, and rolled back onto my elbows, afraid to move.

Nikos squinted at me.

"I think we need to wash up first, Daag. We'll see you at the house in a bit."

"Good," said Daag. "That gives me time to get the glögg going."

"Glögg?"

"Mulled wine," said Nikos.

I mouthed a little *oh* from my supine position, and Nikos took in a long breath through his nose.

"See you, then!" Daag said cheerily and bounded off down the stairs. Nikos kept his eyes on me until we both heard the downstairs door latch shut.

In one step, he was leaning over me, both his fists pressed into the mattress on either side of my hips. I was done for. Any movement, any slight shift, and I was going to burst.

Nikos looked right into my eyes and made no noise whatsoever but for the same calm and measured breathing as the night he'd first kissed me.

After a few minutes of this, I could barely contain myself. I actually whimpered. Only then did Nikos bend his face to mine and brush his lips against my cheek. Then my ear. Then my lips. I moved my head up to kiss him—actually, to eat him alive—but he pulled away and kept moving down along my body, his lips grazing my collarbone, the cloth over one breast, my belly.

When his lips reached the front snap of my trousers, I looked down at him. Nikos grinned and, with his teeth, took hold of the fabric and pulled up, once. *Pop.*

He eased my zipper down and finally used his hands to slide the trousers down to my ankles. I kicked them off. They flew through the air and landed smack against the wall.

Nikos sighed as though he was about to launch into a very serious conversation with whatever it was that was veiled by my string bikini. He slid his middle fingers underneath the sides of my panties, looped the fabric around, then eased them down. And off.

Oh, why didn't women have a mental trick like men did to stop themselves from climaxing too soon? I suppose it was a predicament that a lot of women would kill to be in, that's why. And I was definitely in it deep.

I let my head fall back and looked out the window upside down. There were Willow trees whose green arms swayed in the early evening breeze. A bird flew by. Then another. My thighs were suddenly warm and wet, but I lost track of what got them that way: Nikos's slow-moving mouth or my body's reaction to his slow-moving mouth.

What did it matter? I closed my eyes, hooked my knees over Nikos's shoulders, and let him carry me home.

We hiked along a thin trail through the woods at the back of the house. It was a short trip, and the only words I said were in thanks for holding a tree branch aside for me as we entered the clearing to Daag's yard.

Daag's home was colossal. Nearly twice the size of the "guest" house, this place was of stained wood, with patios that wrapped around both the first and second floors. There was a cupola at the top, and in the back yard a gazebo.

"Did you 'make' this house, too?" I asked.

"A little," said Nikos with a touch of shyness I found completely enchanting.

Nikos rang the front door bell. A fresh-faced, forty-something woman who was about my height answered the door. Her black hair was pulled up in a loose bun and she wore a fitted tunic-and-pants outfit in purple cotton.

"Annika," said Nikos, and he kissed her cheek.

"Welcome, welcome," she said. Her accent was thick Scandinavian. "You must be Norah. Come in, please."

We followed her down the hallway to the living room. It was a similar set-up as the guest house, but much more lived-in. There was an ancient red velvet couch with newspapers and art magazines spread over it. Persian carpets lined the floors, and several of Daag's smaller sculptures rested on shelves and end tables.

Annika cleared a space for us to sit and brought us cups of hot red wine. There was a bowl of walnuts and raisins on the coffee table. Nikos took a spoonful of them and dropped them into his cup. I did the same.

"Daag is lighting the fire out back," said Annika. "We'll go out in a minute."

When she excused herself back to the kitchen, I pulled my legs up underneath me and nestled into the couch.

"Daag's wife is from Gothenburg," said Nikos, picking up one of Daag's plaster sculptures from the bookshelf. "Ever been?"

I shook my head.

He nodded and put the sculpture back. "She's the sweetest woman."

"Seems it," I said.

"You're pretty sweet yourself," Nikos whispered.

"Behave," I whispered back.

Annika returned with a plate of buttery cheese and bread. "It's good to see you again, Nikos. You don't visit so much since the houses are done."

"I know, I know. I've been so busy."

Annika turned to me, her crystal blue eyes smiling. "With you?"

"I'm low- to no-maintenance. I think he means the hotels."

"That reminds me, you're coming to the party, aren't you?" Nikos asked Annika.

"Yes, of course." She took a thoughtful sip of wine. "And Alexis?"

Nikos's face became serious. He lowered himself onto a carpeted ottoman across from me. "He knows when it is. We've been planning this since before the hotels even opened."

Daag came into the living room, and with him came the heady smell of the outdoors. "Bonfire's up. Let's go," he said.

"Are you wearing your boots in the house?" Annika asked, following him out.

I sat there, waiting for Nikos to get up or say something. But he only sat, holding his cup of wine, staring at the floor.

"You want Alexis to be there," I said.

Nikos looked at me somberly. "I wish none of this ever happened. My mother dying, the hitting, the hotels, none of it. I'd still be in Paris."

"I wouldn't have met you," I said, almost to myself.

"Come on," Nikos said, standing. "Daag makes the absolute best bonfires." He put his arm around me and squeezed me to him as we headed out.

The fire was incredible. Ten feet of dead tree branches all leaning in toward each other like a teepee set aflame. We stood around it in the twilight and stared. Annika refilled our cups. I held mine to my nose and let the wine steam rise over my face before taking a warming sip. Every once in a while, Daag poked at the thicker branches to anchor the structure. We could have been standing there for an hour; I lost complete track of time, mesmerized by the heat and the fire licking the air around us.

Nikos stepped behind me and slipped his arms around my shoulders. "Did I lie?"

I leaned back against his chest and shook my head. It was then that I noticed her.

The outer branches had begun to burn away, revealing the center of the fire and what appeared to be the torso of a woman. I blinked. Maybe it was the wine. I blinked again. It was definitely a woman. She leaned urgently forward, her large breasts now crackled embers of bright orange and ash.

I broke free from Nikos and went right up to the fire.

"My god," I said. "There's a woman in there."

"Daag," said Nikos. "What the hell is that?"

"It's me," said Annika. "Or it was supposed to be."

Daag and Annika started to laugh. "My fire goddess," said Daag. "Lately, I've been working in wood instead of plaster," he explained. "Anni posed for me for this sculpture, but—"

"She looked like a big wooden doll," said Annika. "No life."

Daag added, "I thought this was the best way to send her off."

Nikos looked at me and whispered, "Daag doesn't always get the subtleties of symbolism."

I downed the rest of my wine.

"Ready to eat?" asked Annika.

Roast chicken seasoned with fresh basil. Potatoes stewed in basting juices. Fresh garden peas sprayed with lemon. Ice cold well water in a glass pitcher, and an endless decanter of vintage Chianti. I hadn't seen a spread like this in, well, ever.

After all the mulled wine I'd just drunk, I stuck mainly to the water, which I quickly realized was a good thing.

"I am making a toast," said Daag lifting his glass. His cheeks were bright red from the fire and wine and food. "To Nikos. May he return to the world of art, which misses him dearly."

I looked over at Nikos as we clinked glasses. He seemed far away. We began to lower our glasses, but Daag stopped us.

"And! To Norah, his new love." I felt my cheeks flush. "May she be beside him in his return."

"*Skål*," said Annika. We all clinked again.

"Seriously, Nikos," said Daag. "We have to get back to France soon. You're losing your edge."

"Oh, Daag. I'm hurt," said Nikos.

"Look at you. These fine suits you wear. That's not the Nik I know."

"Nik?" I asked. Nikos rolled his eyes at me. "Do you often live out Joni Mitchell songs?" I asked.

"You lost me," Nikos said.

I cleared my throat and sang, "*I was a free man in Paris; I felt unfettered and alive. There was nobody calling me up for favors, no one's future to decide—*"

"It's true!" shouted Daag.

"*You know I'd go back there tomorrow, but for the work I've taken on...* Et cetera and so forth." Annika and Daag applauded, so I toasted them with my water glass.

Nikos stared at me. "I think I just fell in love."

Before I could recover from choking on my water, Daag raised his own glass. "To love," he said. And we all drank to that.

Annika and Daag wouldn't let us help with the clean-up, but I did convince them to let me make coffee. The men went out on the porch to have a smoke. I could hear the low sounds of their conversation over the sink water Annika was running to soak the dishes.

As the coffee finished brewing, Annika took empty cups and a tray of pastries out to the living room. I stepped over to the porch door to call Nikos and Daag inside.

"You're happy," said Daag.

"As much as I can be," said Nikos.

I stood off to the side of the door and smiled to myself.

"I hope you don't mind my saying," Daag spoke in a near whisper, "Norah is much better for you. She understands who you really are, Nik. Not just what your family wanted you to be."

I peeked outside. Nikos exhaled a stream of smoke, but said nothing. I swallowed.

"Paris was wonderful," Daag continued, "but when you and Isobel were together, you were not happy."

"You're wrong," said Nikos. "She was the love of my life."

I sucked in a breath to steady myself and punched the porch screen door open. It flew and smacked hard against the wall of the house.

"Norah? Is everything all right?" asked Daag.

I stared at Nikos with sheer rage. He knew damn well what I'd just heard. He cursed and rushed to put his cigarette out but by that time I was already halfway to the front door.

I think I managed some apology to Annika as I stormed out and broke into a sprint through the darkened back yard toward the trail.

"Norah," Nikos yelled after me.

I wished the houses were miles apart; I just wanted to run and keep running until I collapsed.

"Norah, *wait*, damn it!" He was getting closer.

202

I veered off the path to the guesthouse and leapt over brambles and bent tree branches.

"Go back," I yelled over my shoulder.

I kept my eyes on the glow of the guesthouse's front door lamp as a beacon. Just as I got to the edge of the clearing, Nikos grabbed hold of my arm. I yanked it away from him with a force that could have dislocated my shoulder. I didn't care. I made my legs keep moving toward the house.

"Leave me alo—" Shit. Nikos had the keys. I stopped short. "You lied to me." I began to sob and fell to my knees on the gravel drive. Nikos took a step toward me and I scrambled back up to my feet. "No! I don't want you," I snarled.

My arms ached with the desire to hit something, anything. I picked up a rock from the drive and hurled it at him, but it hit the house instead, smashing a window.

"For god's sake, Norah, please," said Nikos. "Let me talk to you."

"What can you say now? What do you think I'll believe now? You arrogant, hypocritical *shit*." I wiped my mouth. I was seething like a rabid dog. "Let me in the house. I'm calling a cab."

"Fine, let's go in. But before you do anything, let me explain."

Nikos spoke so calmly that it only made me more furious. "I'm going home," I screamed. "Don't come near me."

He walked toward me, intently, and I continued to back up until I tripped over the front steps of the house and fell on my tailbone. Nikos bent down to help me up.

Raging and in pain, I hauled off and took a swing at him. He caught my wrist and held it tight. I saw in his unblinking eyes that he could have, if he'd had the slightest impulse, snapped my arm in two.

I started to bawl like some broken broad in a 1940s gangster film. Nikos scooped me up and took me inside the house. He deposited me on the living room couch without a word and let me cry. When I took my head up out of the pillow I'd been sobbing into, I saw that he'd started a fire in the fireplace.

He sat in front of it, drinking a glass of wine. On the coffee table was the rest of the bottle and another glass.

"How's your ass?" Nikos asked, pouring some wine for me.

I mopped at my face with an afghan that was lying on the back of the couch. I pulled it over my legs.

"It hurts." He nodded and handed me the glass. I took a long sip. "I'm a Wounded Warrior," I said, and started to weep again.

"I see. Is that what your anger says about you?"

"You know the book?"

"Please. When we got to the States, Isobel made me read all of them. Just to be sure I didn't—"

"Why didn't you tell me, Nikos?"

He crawled up onto the couch and took me into his arms. "Isobel was the first person I met when I moved to Paris. I was lonely, and we spent all our time together. I fell in love."

My body jolted as the tears began again. Nikos put his hand across my cheek and began to stroke my face slowly, consolingly, before he continued.

"I settled into my life there, met Daag, got busy with art. Iz and I drifted apart. Our relationship was over before it was over, you know? And then I introduced her to Alexis." He was quiet a minute. "I was going to tell you. Tonight."

"How can I believe that?"

"You have no reason to."

"This was a very big lie." I looked up at him. "I can't trust you now."

"I know."

"I hate that."

"Me, too."

That night we lay, not touching, on the king-sized mahogany four-poster bed. Near dawn, I finally fell asleep. I dreamed I was on fire.

That Tuesday, we were slated to shoot in TriBeCa, at the waterfront. I arrived two hours early, only to find an empty crafts table and a few straggling techies.

"No coffee? What the hell is this? It's already nine-thirty." I'd walked right into Baz's trailer. David was with him. They each held cups of take-out.

"Have a seat, Petal," said Baz. "I've got some bad news."

"Just what I needed," I said. "What's up?"

"The show's been canceled."

I stared open-mouthed at David, who nodded.

"We just got word this morning."

"Why?" I asked, frantic. "Can't we do something?"

"Looks like I already did too much. Greg said sponsors got word about the 'controversial turn' the series had taken and pulled out."

"You're kidding."

"It's my fault," said Baz. "I said I'd leave the show if Smithy didn't come out."

"You didn't," I said.

Baz smiled wanly. "I never thought they'd take little old me so seriously."

"Does Helen know?"

David nodded. "She took the day off to drown her sorrows in old *Handsome Blue* episodes on DVD. I'm taking her out to dinner tonight. Maybe it'll cheer her up." I put a hand on David's shoulder.

"I fell on my ass while trying to kick the crap out of Nikos."

"Delightful. I guess those anger management books were a good investment, eh, Petal?" Baz slapped his legs. "Come tell Daddy all about it."

I parked my ailing tush in his lap and wrapped my arms around his neck. "I don't really want to relive it right now, okay?"

Baz sighed dramatically. "Well, shit, Davey. Looks like we're going to have to play Hollywood Movie Stars again."

"Looks like it," said David.

I sat up. "You're not leaving right away, are you? What about me? And Helen?"

Baz looked over at David, expectantly.

David tried to muster a smile. "Helen's coming back to Los Angeles with us."

"She is?" I whined. I didn't think I had any tears left; I'd been blubbering alone in my apartment since I got back from Daag's place in Hudson.

Baz bumped me up and down on his thigh. "And you, my dumpling? My proposal's still good, you know."

I stared off, picturing myself glamorously tending to Baz on movie sets all over the world. A free woman in Paris. Or Milan. Or Sydney. Or Bombay! If I played my cards right, I could get Baz into the world of Bollywood in no time. They'd eat up a yummy *gora* Brit like him.

I smiled. "Yes, Baz, I accept. I will marry you."

"That's my girl," said Baz, brightening.

Harriet knocked once and opened the trailer door. She processed the sight of me in Baz's lap, then looked immediately at the floor.

"I need to pick up your wardrobe," she mumbled. When she got to the rack of clothing, though, she just stood there, shoulders hunched. "Do you want any of this stuff?" She let out a stifled whimper. "As a keepsake, like?"

"All of it," said Baz.

"Me, too," said David.

"Fine. Less work for me," said Harriet. She buried her face in the outfit that Captain Smithy was supposed to wear today when he announced to his precinct he was a proud, gay cop. "I can't believe this is happening."

"No one can, love," said Baz.

Harriet came over to us, tears welling. "I just want to say good luck, and—" Two fat drops slid down her cheeks as she touched my arm. "—I hope the both of you have a wonderful life together."

I bit my lip. Harriet smiled sadly at David and then stepped down out of the trailer, blowing her nose on a hanky she'd removed from her pocket. The door slammed shut with a tinny clap.

The three of us burst out laughing.

"Oh, fuck me," said Baz, wiping his eyes.

"Enough of the melodramatics," I said, jumping off Baz's lap. "We need serious pampering. David, call your woman. Tell her to get her butt off the couch and meet us at Jean-Francois. Baz?"

"Yes, my bride?"

"Your treat."

"Oh. Right."

Helen was too miserable to mind that we dragged her into work on her day off. Her eyes were so puffy from crying she immediately prescribed herself the FabFrancois Facial. Baz and I ordered up deep tissue massages, and David went off to get his legs waxed.

I didn't ask, but Helen saw the look on my face when David ordered it. As we headed to our respective treatment rooms, she whispered, "At first I thought it was strange, too, but in bed?" She grabbed my arm. "Sexy as shit. Trust me."

By the time I got home, I was vibrating with good energy again. I had opted out of the paraffin wax foot treatment that came with the massage in favor of some reflexology. The technician, a little man named Jin, spent nearly ten minutes kneading the centers of my feet, trying to unblock my stagnant kidney *qi*.

I don't know if it was his treatment that did it or the liter of water I chugged in the cab on the way home, but I had to pee like a racehorse. Once safely on the toilet, I checked my iPhone. One message. When did that come in?

"Norah, it's me. I thought I'd give you a few days to...I don't know."

I plugged my free ear to make sure I got every syllable over the sound of Niagara Falls.

"I hope you know you're still welcome to the party next Friday," said Nikos. "Baz, too. And David, Helen. All of you." There was a pause. "Call me when you get this. If you want."

I sat there. The four of us decided we'd leave for Los Angeles the following Saturday. Technically, we could still make the party. But did I really want to go to a party where I'd certainly see Isobel and Nikos in the same room together? It would be too painful. Better to break the news to him now and spend the rest of my week detoxing.

I parked myself in the hotel lobby and took in the bustling of guests and staff members. There was plenty of time to go up and tell Nikos I was leaving. It wasn't something I was eager to do, anyway.

My attention was caught by a flurry of activity around a set of double doors on the opposite side of the elevators. I'd never noticed them before.

A sign above the doors read: Master Ballroom. A few staff members slipped in an out of them, carrying chairs or stacks of tablecloths. At one point as they were closing, I slipped inside. Tiered floors of red carpeting surrounded a parquet dance floor. Four chandeliers dangled elegantly from the ceiling. There were workers at the top of long ladders, polishing them.

I felt like I'd stepped directly into a fairy tale. That is, until I felt a tap on my shoulder. "Sorry, Miss, this room is off limits," said a suited man carrying a clipboard.

I apologized and backed out just as the elevator opened and I found myself standing right in front of Isobel. I had no idea what to do. But Isobel did. A satisfied grin curled along her lips.

"I warned you, didn't I?" she said. "You simply don't fit in, Norah. Not with our family. Nikos told me he thinks you are very sweet. I am sorry you got hurt."

I could not formulate words. In fact, all the saliva seemed to retreat from my mouth.

"He also said he invited you to our party. I do hope you will be there. So much has happened so quickly." She blinked slowly. "Nik and I have a big announcement to make."

In an instant, I felt the fiery ache of rage in my body. My pulse throbbed in my temples. My fingers twitched. I squeezed them into tight fists, digging fingernails into my palms.

"I should thank you," she continued. "You have really done something to Nikos." Isobel removed a compact from her handbag and checked herself in it. She made no adjustments before returning it to her bag.

I took a step back, tried to control myself. *Don't lose it*, I told myself. *Just turn around and walk away.* I gritted my teeth and pivoted 180-degrees, blocking myself from Isobel's serpentine voice.

"He is so much, how shall I say," Isobel leaned forward and hissed directly into my ear, "*gentler* with me now."

I turned. "That's not all you should thank me for, Isobel. Up until now, I've kept my mouth shut about The Exchange. Wouldn't it be a shame for Nikos to find out what lengths you've gone to just to be sure he couldn't make any decisions for himself?"

Isobel send a stinging smack across my face. Before I realized what was happening, my hand arced around and laid a hard return slap against her ivory cheek. She crumpled like a deflating balloon at the Macy's Thanksgiving Day Parade.

Isobel sat on the ground, stunned, rubbing the side of her face. That was the moment I saw Nikos step out of the elevator doorway. He was staring at me incredulously.

"You *bitch*," Isobel screeched up at me.

"She forced me!" I blurted.

"Bitch," Isobel cried more wretchedly now that Nikos was there.

"Christ, Norah," said Nikos, kneeling at Isobel's head. He propped her up in his lap and called for someone to bring ice.

"I'll get it," I said.

Nikos put up a hand. "Just. Go."

Isobel glared at me. She wasn't nearly as hurt as she was making out.

"But she—" I began, voice quavering.

"Norah," Nikos interrupted. "Now."

"I came here to tell you that I'm moving to Los Angeles," I said. "So I guess I'll miss your big announcement."

"Good fucking riddance," said Isobel.

Nikos shushed her and lifted his eyes to mine. I held them only for a second before I turned and ran out, bumping into staff members who were rushing with ice and towels to clean up the second mess I'd left on the floor of the Hotel Ursula.

There was no question in my mind that no one, not even Helen, was going to be able to stop the depression I was sinking into. Upon arriving home, I didn't even bother to stop by Helen's to tell her what I'd done. Instead, I mechanically stripped off my clothes, leaving a trail of them from the front door to the bedroom.

I put on my old nightgown, grabbed the box of tissues from the bathroom and two unopened boxes from the closet. I crawled in bed and pulled the covers up to my eyes.

Then the head torture started.

Nikos tucked you into this very bed. But that was when he cared.

I squeezed my eyes shut, but I saw his face everywhere. The anonymous Man in White, stepping off the elevator.

Imagine; there was a time you didn't even know his name.

Nikos at the art gallery, smiling with surprise when he realized I was there.

Flirtatious Nikos in his car, in the rain.

Silent Nikos sitting next to me on my couch, staring at the candlelight.

Nikos, aroused and expectant, from between my legs.

Then, his voice came. The intimate, sleepy baritone asking me to dinner, sharing the story of his life, telling us all at the dinner table that he'd just fallen in love...

I had failed. My stupid rage had cost me the best thing I'd ever have. I was in a tailspin. And no one was there to catch me.

Sometime later I woke up. I didn't remember falling asleep. In fact, I had no idea what time or even what day it was.

Helen sat on the edge of my bed. I'm sure I looked like a latter scene from *The Exorcist*, without the green puke. I was in fetal position, unwashed, unfed, and surrounded by a mound of tissues. They were old and hardened now. At some point, I must have switched to bath towels; there were two of them in my clutches, wadded up like security blankets.

Helen had the courage to reach over and tuck my greasy hair behind one ear. The physical contact made me launch into a new fit of sobbing. Helen joined me.

"I'm sorry, Norah," she said as she wept.

"Don't be. I'm a monster." I blew my nose into a towel.

"I was so worried about you. I've been sleeping on the couch."

"How long?"

"About three days," Helen said, wiping her face.

"Oh, god," I wailed, remembering everything. "Of all the things I could do to Isobel! She's an abuse survivor, Helen, and I *hit* her." I could barely catch my breath. "You should have seen the look on Nikos's face when he saw her lying on the floor. I might as well have ripped his heart out with my teeth."

"What can I do?" asked Helen.

"Put me out of my misery. I mean it. Smother me with a pillow. Make me a Valium cocktail. I am not fit for human consumption."

"Stop it," Helen cried. "I can't stand to hear you talk like this."

"Then leave," I yelled. "I didn't ask you to come. Just leave me alone."

"I can't." Helen was bawling. "I'm afraid."

"Of what?"

"Of you," she said. "Of what you'll do. We all are. Baz is a wreck. He can't find his nail clippers. I bought him some but he said they hurt his cuticles," Helen cried harder. "Even David's completely messed up. We haven't made love in hours."

She grabbed one of my two towels and covered her face with it. "I've never seen you like this. If anything happens to you," she collapsed, her head landing in my lap, "I'll be alone. I won't know what to do. We need you, Norah."

I reached down and placed my hand on Helen's cheek. It was the same thing Nikos had done to soothe me that night at the guesthouse. How grounding his touch was, how safe it made me feel. After a while, Helen's sobs reduced to occasional hiccups. I kept stroking her exactly the way Nikos had done to me: Cheek to ear, cheek to ear, a few fingers lingering through the hair. It was reassuring somehow, as though he were here with me again.

Helen sat up. "I have something for you."

She went into the living room and returned with a plastic bag. She handed it to me. Inside was a brand new DVD of *Devdas*, a wildly popular remake of a 1955 Bollywood classic that, despite it having been released years ago, I had yet to add to my collection.

"I returned your old rentals and told the guy at the store that you were sick and how much you like that Khan guy. He got all confused." Helen sniffled. "Evidently there's more than one Khan guy?"

"Four or five."

"Yeah, anyway. He gave me this. Is he the right one?"

"I like this Khan guy just fine," I slid the DVD back in the bag. "Come here, you."

Helen sat down next to me and I hugged her. "Thanks, Hel. For everything."

"Well, shit," she said. "You'd do the same for me."

"Doubt it. Not if you smelled as bad as I do right now."

Helen pulled away. "I wasn't going to say anything, but, *whew*! I'm setting you up on a date with Mr. Shower."

I flipped the covers off me, stood up, and immediately sat back down again. "Hm. I think I need a date with Mr. Sandwich first."

"There's some Mr. Leftover Pizza in the fridge." Helen headed out to the kitchen.

"I think I just fell in love," I said, cheerily. Then Nikos's voice echoed the words in my head and my stomach turned.

Hooray For Bollywood

Cold pizza and a hot shower will do wonders for a woman.

Once she was sure I wasn't going to off myself in the tub, Helen went back across the hall to make up for lost time with David. She confiscated my bottle of Tylenol PM and, for some reason, my Lady Bic.

I wandered dreamily around the bedroom in my best self-esteem-building French blue silk robe, tossing away the tissue mountain, putting the snotty towels in the hamper, stripping the bed, remaking it.

I felt good. Purged. But not purged enough.

My favorite old nightgown lay wadded up in a corner of the room. The very sight of it made me ill now. I picked it up with two fingers and tossed it into the garbage with the tissues.

Then I headed into the living room and unplugged the iPhone from its charger. Voicemail. Of course I have voicemail. Screw it.

The thought that some of them, even one of them, could have been Nikos sent my stomach fluttering again. I gave myself a good hard punch, right in the flutter.

Stop it. No more. I'm sick to death of your girlie little weak-kneed crap, Norah. Get tough. You know how to do that, don't you?

"Yes!" I answered, raising a triumphant finger. Then I brought that finger down and hit the power button, shutting the phone down.

There was a bouquet of wildflowers on the coffee table with a note: "You don't have to get back on the horse if you don't want to. Love, H."

Good thing, too. I had wicked saddle sores and no intention of going anywhere near the stables again for a while.

I nestled into the couch with a glass of Shiraz and popped in *Devdas*, starring Shah Rukh Khan. He was no Aamir, but he definitely fell into the eye candy category. Besides, when it first came out, there was a lot of buzz about this movie being a breakthrough in Bollywood love stories. This new millennium *Devdas* promised to be a twist on the typical theme of inter-class, star-crossed lovers; it was a love triangle extraordinaire.

Three hours later, my head still swimming from the colors and the music and the dancing and the angst of unrequited love, I was banging on Helen's door. When I tried the handle, it opened.

She must have been in such a hurry to get her jellyroll filled, she never locked it.

"Helen! I've got it!" I ran right to her bedroom. She and David were fast asleep. I leapt up onto the foot of the bed and jumped up and down. "It was all right there in the movie!"

Helen groaned. "Jesus, I should have left you the Tylenol PM."

"What time is it?" David asked, his head wedged under his pillow.

"Listen to me," I said. I got off the bed and knelt at the foot. "Are you listening?"

Helen sat up and folded her hands in her lap. "What."

"She doesn't love him."

"Great. You can give me a detailed film review in the morning. Good night."

"No! *Isobel.* She doesn't love Nikos. Not really."

David pulled the pillow off his head.

"See, in the movie, Devdas and Paro are childhood sweethearts. Devdas goes to London to study and comes back ten years later. Now Paro is all grown up and beautiful, but very vain. Anyway, they fall in love, but Dev's father forbids him to marry her, so she gets married off to this older man—"

"I'm lost," sighed Helen.

"Hang on. On the day of her wedding, Devdas breaks into her chambers and asks her to elope with him. He tells her she's beautiful, like the moon. Paro says she's more beautiful; the moon is scarred. She secretly still loves him, but she's pissed off that he wouldn't stand up to his father."

"I still don't see what this has to do with Nikos and Isobel and the brother—"

"He hits her!" I exclaimed, pounding my fists on the bed. "With tears in his eyes, Devdas takes this big string of wedding pearls from her hands like he's just trying to touch anything that's hers one last time, but out of nowhere he whips it around and brings it clear across her forehead. Leaves a little gash right here." I pointed to my hairline.

"Lord."

"Then he says, 'I have scarred you like the moon with the mark of my love.'" I melted onto the mattress. "Isn't that just the sexiest thing you've ever heard?"

"I seriously worry for you."

"Dev ends up living with a courtesan who he never lets touch him. Then he drinks himself to death. The point is that Paro is only with this older man as a distraction—the way Isobel is with Nikos! Deep in her heart, Paro-Isobel still loves Devdas-Alexis—*even though he hurt her*. Get it?"

Helen chewed on her lip for a moment. "So, now what?"

"Now, I bring Devdas to Paro before he hooks up with some Parisian whore and dies of alcohol poisoning." I stood up and tightened my robe. "Nothing can stand in the way of true love, Helen. Isobel and Alexis were meant to be together. They just need a little help."

"So, are you the courtesan?" asked David, half-asleep.

Helen pulled the pillow back over his head and looked me over with more concern than I thought necessary. "Hon, you've had a rough few days. Why don't you go to sleep and see if you still think it's a good idea in the morning."

"There's no time. It's already Thursday morning. The party is Friday night. I have so much to do!"

"Great. I'll visit you in the nuthouse," Helen yelled, but I was already out the door.

From: Norah Pasquale <norahnyc@hotmail.com>
To: Alexis Santos <asantos@santoshotels.com>
Subject: Santos Family Gala
Date: Thu, October 29, 2.16 am

Dear Mr. Santos:

 I am writing on behalf of your brother, Nikos, to request your presence at the Santos Family Gala on Friday, October 31 at the Hotel Ursula in New York City.

 Please forgive the short notice, however, the fact that you have been out of touch with Nikos has made it difficult for me to locate you. Now that I have, I can only hope that over these many years you have come to share your brother's hope that the time has come to end the unfortunate silence between you.

 What better way to do that than by celebrating with your only sibling the gift that your mother left to you? At your word, I will see to all the necessary arrangements.

  Most sincerely yours,
  Norah Pasquale
  Personal Assistant to Nikos Santos

P.S. I am sure you are wondering about Isobel. She will be there. Please: Come for her, too.

I was doing a mitzvah. At least that's what I convinced myself as I scoffed down three consecutive slices of pizza, standing at the kitchen counter, nearly apoplectic with the realization that I could have just royally screwed up.

Belly full, I forced myself to get into bed and try to sleep. I couldn't. But why not? My motives were pure. It wasn't about getting Nikos back anymore, was it?

Maybe it was the pizza.

The next afternoon, I had a date with Baz. He wanted to West Coastify me before our big trip. This would involve a new wardrobe of "non-dreary" color schemes and accessories appropriate to the PA of a major motion picture icon. I assumed that meant a dainty cellphone and hot pink walkie-talkies.

Before I left the house, I checked my email. Nothing. This worried me immensely. Paris was five hours ahead, which meant it was already evening there. Surely Alexis would have read my email by now. He must have decided not to answer.

"Of course, he could be on a bender," Baz offered on our cab ride to upper Madison Avenue.

"Not helpful but, sadly, quite possible. All thanks to my little note, I'll bet."

I had told Baz about my epiphany and, for the first time in my life, I asked his opinion of the situation.

"It is bold, I'll say that. And definitely romantic, which is always good," said Baz. "There's one thing you never mentioned, though. Why did Alexis hit Isobel?"

"Does it matter?"

"Well, yes. Did she just get lippy with him or was she, oh, perhaps, shagging his brother on the side?"

"Jesus, Baz, I'm trying to give my tear ducts a rest. Could you please not put horrible thoughts like that into my mind?"

"Stop right here," Baz told the cab driver. "Never mind. I'm sure you'll hear from your Devdas." He paid the driver and we stepped out onto Seventy-fourth Street. "Now forget about those hot-blooded ethnic men and pay attention to pasty old Anglican me. It is time to shop for your trousseau."

"This wedding metaphor is becoming unhealthy, Baz."

"Face it, Petal." Baz looped his arm through mine. "I'm never going to get married. Let me play."

"Yeah, well, the only aisle I'll be walking down anytime soon will be the one on the plane to California."

Baz stopped.

"Whatever is that very strange look on your face, Basil?"

"Let's get married."

"You really know how to kick a girl when she's down."

"I mean it. It'll be brilliant! Like Matt Damon and his assistant."

"They didn't get married, and she was Ben Affleck's assistant, not his. Personal assistants don't marry their movie stars. It would blow a hole in the entire caste system."

"And what's so wrong with blowing a few holes?"

I started walking again. "I'm swept off my feet. Really."

"Just think about it."

"In case it hadn't occurred to you, Baz, there's also the small matter of our incompatible sexual preferences."

"Please. Do you want a list of gay-straight unions throughout history based on the same thing?"

"No."

"Oscar Wilde, for one. Tchaikovsky, Rock Hudson, Cole Porter—"

"*No*, Baz."

"Tom Cruise."

"Basil! Stop!"

"Anyway, I'm ambisexual, as you know but clearly do not believe." Baz sighed. "Fine. When we're done here we'll go back to your place and fuck like bunnies."

Baz steered me up the steps of an ivy-walled red brick building that had been converted into a consignment shop. He waved to a middle-aged, well-pressed woman behind the counter.

"Gertie! Hullo, love. This is my fiancée, Norah—"

"Baz! I mean it!" I gave his upper arm a hard thwack with the back of my hand.

"We're having our first spat," he said.

"First? Ha."

"Don't worry, dear," said Gertie in a thick Northern English accent, "I've known this old tart too long. He can't pull anything over on me. Now, what d'you need?"

Baz ran down the list of all the possible Hollywood events I'd be attending over the next six months—business lunches, press dinners, awards ceremonies, charity balls...

"Yes," I interrupted. "I need a gown. A show-stopping, room-silencing, drop-dead incredible piece of work. For the off-chance I may attend a charity ball-type-of-thing in the near future."

Baz rolled his eyes. "I know what you're up to, Ms. Pasquale. And if you think for one instant that I'm going to fund an outfit that will only be used to woo the only man you love more than me—" Baz took one look at my face and resignedly slapped his credit card into Gertie's pink palm. "Give her the works, Gert." He slapped me on the backside. "I'm going back to the hotel to sulk."

"Oh, no you're not," I said. "I need you here to tell me how beautiful I look."

He slumped into a settee. "Do I have to?"

"That's what good husbands do," said Gertie.

I nodded, ruefully. "I'd hate to have your job."

Gertie gave me a once-over then clapped her hands together. "I have just the thing."

She bustled off and called to me from the back of the shop. "Try this on, love," she said.

Hanging there in the dressing room was a long, strapless gown in red satin with more personality than I could ever hope to have.

"It'll probably need some taking in around the bust," Gertie said, eyeing my chest. "And you don't have much in the way of hips, do you, dear?"

"I manage to keep my pants on," I said defensively.

"Never mind. Just give 'er a slip on and we'll see where we are."

Once I'd gotten into the gown, I stepped out of the dressing room with a frown. Gertie was right. The dress sagged in front and swam around my hips. "I look like I'm trying on my mother's party dress."

"Not for long," Gertie said, slipping the bifocals that had been hanging from a gold chain around her neck up onto her nose. She began pulling at the gown, pinning all the loose material together.

"Do I have enough boob to pull this off?" I asked, yanking the top of the dress up.

"Don't muss about," said Gertie. "By the time I'm done, you're going to be filling out of the top of this dress like the head on a Guinness stout."

"I find it hard to believe I have enough flesh up here to fill a shotglass."

Gertie stopped her hemming and looked at me over the tops of her glasses. "Sweetie, I can't tell you how many flat-chested starlets I've puffed up for the Academy Awards." She resumed her pinning. "Half of them waste their money on silicone when all they need is a good seamstress."

She stood and grabbed the gown between my shoulder blades. "Watch," she said, giving it a yank. Two half moons of milky white breast presented themselves at the top of the gown.

I smiled. "Well, hello there."

"Leave it to Gertie, my darling. Now, let's go give old Bazzer a thrill."

She pinned me in place and I stepped out to the front of the shop. Baz had a pink feather boa around his neck and was filing though a rack of silk blouses.

"Ahem," I said.

He turned around and his jaw unhinged. He blinked a few times.

"You've got *tits*," he said, finally.

"I have to return them by midnight or they turn into pumpkins."

"Gertie, you've outdone yourself," said Baz.

"This is nothing," she said, ushering me back to the dressing room. "Take off the dress and mind the pins, dear."

"When will it be ready?" I asked.

"Do you need it right away?"

I bit my lip. "Tomorrow night."

Gertie sighed. "I'd better get sewing then, hadn't I?"

Oh, Brother, Where Art Thou?

I returned home at six o'clock and immediately turned on my computer. Oh, I was well aware that on the surface it appeared insane that I should be going through all this trouble to reunite a woman with her abuser, but I held firm to my Devdas theory. True love would prevail. At least I hoped so. If Alexis hadn't responded by now, I'd have my answer.

One message was in my mailbox.

From: *Alexis Santos*
Subject: *Re: Santos Family Gala*

I closed my eyes and said a small prayer. Then I opened the message, took one look, and moaned out loud. I picked up the phone.

"Helen?" I said, trying to remain calm, "Can you come over here pronto?"

"Sure thing. What's going on?"

"I'll tell you when you get here. And if you happen to have one lying around, bring a French dictionary."

As soon as I hung up, Helen was at the door.

"Where's the dictionary?"

"Ta-dah," she said, ushering David into the living room.

"You speak French?"

"*Oui*," said David. "Picked it up on a film shoot."

"Picked it up? You don't pick up French on a film shoot. Herpes, maybe, but not an entire language."

"David's brilliant. He's like a Swiss Army knife," Helen said, beaming, "only a *guy*."

I took David to the computer and sat him down to read.

"Why would Alexis respond in French? What is that?" I asked Helen.

"I don't know, maybe he just assumed."

"Or maybe he's an arrogant weenie."

"Well," said David, "He's coming." I sat down on the edge of the couch. "In fact, he's already gotten his ticket. He'll be here tomorrow morning at eight."

I stood at the international arrival gate of JFK's Terminal 1 with a cluster of livery drivers. In my hand was a white placard that read: SANTOS.

As passengers ambled through the glass doors, I tried to play it cool—not to search their faces expectantly—but after fifteen minutes, my palms began to sweat.

What if David read the message wrong? What if Alexis missed his flight? What if he thought it was just some cruel joke Isobel was playing on him and *that* was why he'd responded in French? I lowered the card. Boy, I messed up. As it was, I was going to have to explain using the studio car and driver a week after the show was canceled. I felt sick.

And then I saw him. There was no question that the vision of expertly tailored manliness heading toward me was Alexis Santos. My lord, this family's gene pool was the Homo sapiens equivalent of the Fertile freaking Crescent.

Alexis was tall, but not as tall as Nikos, and more angular. His hair was deep chestnut, just like his brother's, but he wore it short, with just a few wisps curling down over his forehead. He had a leather overnight case on one shoulder and a tuxedo bag flung over the other.

As his long slow strides brought him closer to me, I saw the trademark chiseled cheekbones, the full lips, striking eyes. But Alexis's were hazel, not dark like Nikos's, and at the moment they were searching for something.

I found the presence of mind to hold the placard back up and readjust my stupefied expression before Alexis turned his gaze on me.

"You are Norah?" he asked in a voice like melted butter. Figured.

I nodded like a chipper cruise director.

"Mr. Santos. Welcome to New York. Do you have any luggage?"

Alexis, apparently tickled by the official treatment, lifted the bags from his shoulders and gave them a jaunty shake. He was delightful. I only hoped I wasn't drooling.

Only one thing to do: I imagined wiping his butt.

That did the trick.

I escorted him to the car and got in next to him.

"So, Nikos has a personal assistant," Alexis said as we pulled out onto the highway. "He must be doing well."

I smiled politely. "Are you looking forward to seeing him again?"

"No," said Alexis, lighting a Marlboro. "I am more, how should I say, scared shitless."

He wasn't the only one.

"But I suppose if he invited me, that means he is not planning to kill me."

I looked out the window. Light traffic. We would be at the Hotel Ursula in less than an hour. I had no idea how I was going to get Alexis inside without Nikos seeing him. Or me for that matter. There hadn't been time to think it all through.

I took out my cell phone and dialed. "Mr. Vancouver?"

"Norah," Baz sighed. "Just because you won't marry me doesn't mean you have to revert to formalities."

"Yes, hello. I'm calling to reconfirm Mr. Alexis Santos's reservation...in the *Presidential Suite*."

Alexis looked over at me with surprise. I gave him a perky thumbs-up.

"You got Alexis? He's there?" Baz asked, breathless.

"That's right."

Baz said something to someone else in the room. "Don't worry about a thing, Petal. Davey and I are on it."

"David's there?"

Alexis tried to cover his puzzlement over my suddenly familiar tone by rooting around in the front flap of his bag.

"Ah, David, the concierge. Well, that's fine. We'll be there in approximately twenty minutes."

"Twenty minutes? Damn, we were just having a Jacuzzi."

"*Twenty minutes.*" I leaned as close to the window as I could and whispered, "I have two words for you: Housekeeping. *Now.*"

I clicked off and smiled at Alexis.

"You run a tight ship," he said, impressed. "My brother must absolutely love you."

My heart was somewhere in the vicinity of my tonsils as the car dropped Alexis and me off in front of the Hotel Ursula. Alexis got out and looked around as I quickly grabbed his bags from the trunk.

I rushed past Alexis to the front doors. There were dozens of staff members running around, but no sign of Nikos. The place looked incredible. Ice sculptures were being wheeled into the hotel. Red carpeting and ornate oil lamps lined the walk. You'd think Nikos was hosting the Oscars.

Alexis followed slowly behind me, taking it all in. When we stepped into the lobby, Baz and David greeted us. But before I could say a word, Baz gave me a silencing look.

"Mr. Santos?" he said in his television voice, perfect gritty New York cop.

Alexis stiffened. "Yes."

Baz pulled aside his jacket revealing his badge and a flash of his packed shoulder holster. Alexis looked like he was going to bolt.

"I'm Captain William Smithy and this is Lieutenant Daniel Dawson, NYPD."

David nodded once and showed his badge.

"Is there something wrong, *officers*?" I asked.

"Not at all, Ma'am. We're here for Mr. Santos's protection. We've secured the area so we can to escort Mr. Santos to his quarters without incident." He stressed the last two words for my benefit.

"It that really necessary?" Alexis asked me. I blinked, speechless.

Baz angled his head toward the elevators. "You have to understand, Mr. Santos," he explained as we walked. "Tonight's event has been highly publicized. You're a very important man. We don't want to take any risks with your safety."

"You don't watch American television, do you?" I whispered to Alexis.

"I do not have a television. Why?"

"Never mind. Good," I said. "That's very good."

Baz opened the doors of the Presidential Suite. It was immaculate. In better shape than I'd seen it since Baz moved in. There was even a fresh fruit basket on the coffee table.

"This is incredible," Alexis said. "I cannot believe what he has done with this place."

"Me, either," I said in Baz's direction. He winked at me. I put Alexis's bag down on the valet stand. "Can I get you anything before I go?"

"No," Alexis said in a daze, fingering the frame of a high-back antique chair. "Wait, yes. I would like to see Isobel."

"Sure thing, sir," Baz said.

I shot Baz a look of death.

"At the party tonight," Baz recovered. "You can see her then. And your brother. But right now they're, uh—"

"At lunch," David said to Baz. He was standing at military ease. "Sir."

"Together?" asked Alexis, his voice rising.

I was afraid he'd lunge at Baz if he didn't get the answer he wanted. Hiding behind Alexis's tux bag, I made a surreptitious head shake in Baz direction.

"No," said Baz. "I believe Mr. Santos went out alone."

Alexis took a banana from the fruit basket and leaned back into the chair with a sigh. He stared at the piece of fruit, then put it back and lit up a Marlboro.

"I'm sure you're exhausted. Try to get some rest," I said. "I'll come back to get you for the party."

"Either Lieutenant Dawson or myself will be right outside if you need anything," said Baz.

Alexis nodded distantly as the three of us stepped out and Baz closed the door. Without a word, I pointed to the stairwell.

"What's going on?" I asked once we were safely behind the fire door.

"Isn't this fun?" Baz squealed, clapping his hands.

"We'll keep him in the room," said David, "and we can make sure Alexis doesn't see Isobel—"

"—or Nikos," Baz added. "Until you give the word."

I pulled them both into a hug. "You sneaky actor-types," I said. "Thank you." I released them. "Where's Helen?"

David took out his cell phone. "She already picked up your dress. All you have to do now is go home and get ready. She's waiting for my call."

"Leave everything else to us," said Baz. He gave me a quick squeeze. "It's show time, Petal."

Helen had a hot herbal bath and a shot of Scotch waiting for me when I got home. I downed the shot and submerged myself in the tub.

She sat on the toilet lid, brushing out a hair extension. "So what's he like?"

I spoke through the lavender-scented washcloth she'd draped over my face. "Alexis? The *GQ* version of Nikos. Young, dark, fashionable, brooding."

"Yummy."

"Seriously yummy."

"You know," Helen said reflectively, "Nikos means so much to you and I've never seen him. Except for that online pic."

I took the washcloth off my face.

"I was thinking that it might be fun if I, you know, came with you tonight. You're under a lot of stress, I realize that, but maybe if I were there—"

"Helen, do you really want to see Nikos or do you just want to go to The Big Party?"

Helen lay the extension across her lap. "I want to see Nikos...at The Big Party."

"You're so transparent," I said covering my face again.

"Bitch."

"Loser."

"Well?"

"Well, of course you're coming with me, you dope. You think I'm going to take this giant leap into the abyss without my best friend there for moral support?"

Helen jumped up. "I know exactly what I'm going to wear!"

"I'm sure you do."

"Come on, get your tush out of that tub. There's hardly enough time to get us both ready."

Helen and I stood before each other, grinning like high school prom queens. She was in a black sequined gown and fine lace gloves. Her hair was twisted into an up-do held by a rhinestone-encrusted comb.

As for my red satin gown, no matter what I did, or how I moved, the dress hugged me. It was like a hundred little hands working to urge my body into all the right places. God bless Gertie.

She had even thrown in a pair of matching shoes: T-straps with slender heels that finished out the look perfectly. I felt at least a foot taller. Especially with the hair extension Helen had expertly hid on the top of my head under my own locks. They flowed together and fell over my shoulders in loose curls.

"You could be a Bond girl," said Helen, turning me around.

"I feel light-headed. Maybe the dress is too tight."

"You're just nervous. But don't be. I have a very good feeling about tonight."

My cell phone began to sing its Rolling Stones ditty.

"Norah Pasquale," I said.

"Petal, we have a problem," said Baz.

I rolled my eyes at Helen and covered the mouthpiece. "You had to jinx it, didn't you?"

"What did I say?"

"What's happening, Baz?"

"We've lost him."

"You lost Alexis?" I whimpered.

"Oh, no," said Helen, leaning against the kitchen counter.

"How, Baz? I thought you were right outside his door."

"He's not under hotel arrest, you know. He said he wanted to get some air."

"Is Nikos there? What if he sees him? Shit. I'm coming over."

"When we get to the hotel," I told Helen in the cab, "I need you to keep an eye out for Nikos or Isobel. If you see either of them, call my cell immediately and let me know exactly where they are so I can keep Alexis away. If I can even find him."

Helen put her hand on mine. "Relax."

"I can't. If either of them sees Alexis before the party, my whole plan will be ruined."

"But wasn't your plan to get them together again? If they see each other, then they'll be together again."

"I need to be there as a buffer."

"Do you?"

I looked at Helen. "What are you saying?"

"Remember what I told you about having a goal firmly in your mind and sticking to it?"

"That's exactly what I'm doing."

Helen shook her head. "I love you, Norah, but you're lying to yourself. This isn't some magnanimous thing you're doing to reunite a family. You're in love with Nikos and you're fighting to get him back."

I tried to protest, but Helen put up a hand. "That's not a criticism. It's admirable, honey. Own it."

"What if it doesn't work and Nikos thinks I'm a fool?"

"I think you already know the answer to that."

"Yeah, yeah. He's the fool, blah, blah."

"One of the biggest mistakes women make is giving men control they're not even asking for. We just roll over on our backs and hope they'll like us. Go for what you want, Norah. You're at war. Take no prisoners."

"Can I take one?"

"Nikos isn't a prisoner. Technically, he's a spoil of war."

"Oh." I sighed and hoisted my boobs in my gown. "This conversation is weird."

"Yeah." Helen sighed. "I'm so nervous for you."

We stepped out of the car, directly into a mass of paparazzi I hadn't anticipated. Helen, being Helen, lapped it up, slipping effortlessly into Star Mode. She lifted her chin, lowered her sunglasses and winked at the photographers.

I, however, had another mission. Hanging my head low, I scoped the area for any sight of the Santos gene pool and/or their significant Parisian other.

Halfway up the red carpet, with cameras flashing all around us, we were met by the dually-tuxedoed Baz and David.

"Come on, the party's already started," Baz told me, taking my arm and simultaneously waving to the photohogs.

"Baz! Norah!" called out one of the reporters. "When's the wedding?"

Baz smiled and waved again, pretending not to hear. He whispered into my ear, "There's no sign of Alexis anywhere."

"And Nikos? Isobel?"

"They're holding court inside the ballroom. As long as Alexis didn't get in there—"

"He didn't," David said, holding the door open for Helen. "I checked."

"Good work, officers," I said.

Just as we entered the lobby, a peal of screams came from behind us. There in the doorway, was Baz's boy toy Gio from the Rihga. But this time he had a gun, and it was pointed right at Baz.

"Freeze, you two-timing jerkoff," he yelled.

Baz still had my arm when he turned to face Gio. Instinctively, I stepped in front of Baz, but he took a firm hold of my waist and heaved me aside. He walked directly up to Gio and stood within a foot of his gun barrel. "Poor boy. Did I forget to give you your autograph?"

"You think I'm going to let you marry that fag hag?" bleated Gio. "Well, fuck that."

Someone else screamed, and before anyone saw what was happening, David was behind the kid, his prop gun pressed against Gio's temple.

"Fuck *this*," David whispered in his ear.

Gio stiffened. He was still playing tough, but it was obvious he was freaked. "Who are you?"

"I'm Batman," David said. Gio lowered his gun. "But you can call me Lieutenant Daniel Dawson." David clasped a pair of handcuffs from the back of his tux trousers around the boy's wrists. "You're under arrest."

"My hero," said Baz with a wry smile.

Baz kicked open the front doors and David hurled the kid outside. He toppled down the steps and onto the red carpet. David patted his pockets. "Oh, fudge." He turned to us with a big grin. "I guess I lost the key."

Helen was practically quivering as she threw herself into his arms. Baz let the doors shut, leaving the poor lad to be stoned to death by paparazzi flash bulbs.

"Now," said Baz, "Where were we?"

"Wait a second. Didn't you say Alexis needed some air?" I headed for the elevator.

As I stepped out onto the roof, it took me a minute to recognize this as the same view from the Internet photo I'd seen Nikos in. Only now a different Santos leaned against the railing.

His back was to me, hunched over in his tux. Although his face was turned away, I knew Alexis had been crying. I assumed it was one of the reasons he didn't turn around as soon as he felt my presence.

"Thought we'd lost you."

Alexis glanced out of the corner of his eye. Then he turned full around and gave me a once-over. "Wow."

"Yeah, I clean up good."

"You look more like a princess than a personal assistant."

"About that. I'm not. I mean, I am a PA. Just not Nikos's."

"Then how do you know him?"

"I promise everything will make sense after we go down to the party."

Alexis ran a palm over one of his damp cheeks. "I am not going."

"If you don't mind my saying, you're a little overdressed for hanging out on the roof."

"I thought I could face Isobel, but I cannot. I am so ashamed." He bent his head and two tears slid from his long dark lashes and disappeared a few floors beneath us. Just like a broken-hearted Bollywood hero.

"Maybe if you tell me what happened. It might help."

Alexis drew in a deep breath and straightened. "Well, when I... When she..." His eyes searched the air as though somewhere in it he could find the words he needed. "I cannot say it."

"Okay," I put a hand on his shoulder. "Then why don't I tell you why *I* hit Isobel."

Alexis's lips fell open with surprise. "You?"

"It's despicable, I know. I have no excuse."

"You. Hit Isobel?"

"This is what I'm saying. Do you want to hear why?"

"Dying to."

I looked Alexis dead in the eyes and spoke slowly. I wanted to be sure he heard every word.

"I'm in love with your brother." I paused. I hadn't admitted that to anyone before, not even myself. I half expected angels to start singing. Or the earth to open and swallow me up. But I didn't get so much as an eyebrow flinch from Alexis.

"I love Nikos so much that the very thought of Isobel touching him made me crazy." I sighed. "Of course, now he won't speak to me."

Alexis regarded me for a few resonating moments before turning his face away again. I thought for sure he was crying. He wasn't. He was laughing.

"My heart is broken over here. Can you tell me what's so funny?"

"You are amazing." Alexis shook his head in wonderment. "I do not know how you did it, but you just read my mind."

"Occupational hazard. It's the curse of the personal assistant."

"I never got over the fact that Nikos and Isobel were lovers. It was over long before she and I met; she kept telling me that. But the closer the time came for us all to leave for New York, the more I began to think she only wanted to go because she was looking for an excuse to be with him again.

"When I told her we should not go, that I will stay in Paris with her, she panicked. She said she would die if she could not go to New York." He looked at me. "It was then I knew it was not over between her and Nikos."

"Did you ask him?"

"I was too jealous by then. I hate what I did to her. It makes me sick every day."

Alexis reached into his pocket. "On the morning Isobel left, I found this on her pillow."

He opened his hand. Glistening there in his palm was the same diamond ring I'd seen Isobel wearing in the newspaper photo. Up close, the ring seemed displaced, lonely.

I cupped his fingers around the ring. "Don't you think it's time give this back to her?" Alexis pocketed it. "Come on," I said, offering him my elbow. "We'll go down together."

Alexis gave a quiet laugh. "We just might." He slipped his arm through mine and we headed inside.

I kept up a strong face for Alexis, but my stomach was in triple knots as we headed toward the ballroom. David, Baz, and Helen were waiting by the doors. Helen gave my hair a little poofing as we passed.

"Alexis is disturbingly hot," she whispered in my ear.

I made big, *that's not helping* eyes at her.

"Good luck," said Baz.

"We're right behind you," chirped Helen.

The ballroom floor was flooded with elegant socialites in gowns and tuxes. The hum of lively conversation mingled with clinking of champagne flutes, and everything seemed to be held afloat by the sultry energy of the live jazz combo that played onstage.

Alexis and I headed right down the center of the room to our target. Nikos appeared completely at ease in his spectacular tuxedo. I had a feeling, though, that this was one of those moments he longed for his old chinos. Isobel was predictably astonishing in a black floor-length gown. Her slender-heeled shoes, however, must not have been the best choice for maneuvering the levels of the ballroom floor, because she took Nikos's arm as he helped her down a few steps.

When he laid eyes on Isobel, Alexis sucked in a breath and tightened his grip on my elbow.

"You're fine. They haven't seen us yet. Get yourself together. And Alexis," I added, "No crying." Alexis nodded quickly.

Now we were headed right toward each other: Alexis and me and Nikos and Isobel. Guests had begun to notice the migration, happily making room for us, turning to whisper excitedly to each other about the estranged brother now returned.

When the sea of guests finally parted, it was Isobel who saw us first. Rather, she saw Alexis. She gasped and dropped Nikos's arm as though it were on fire.

A very good sign.

Turning presumably to see what gave Isobel such a start, Nikos finally laid his eyes on me. His lips parted in shock. It was probably my unexpected presence, but I hoped it was more the sensation of my unquestionably fabulous appearance.

Then he saw who was on my arm. Nikos's face became deadly serious. After that, his eyes stayed glued on Alexis.

The room went silent as the four of us stood facing each other. Isobel was having difficulty breathing, and her eyes filled with tears. She tore them away from her husband's face only long enough to regard his hand. It was still holding my arm.

I disengaged Alexis and gave his hand a clandestine, reassuring squeeze as I dropped it.

"So, Isobel," I said, smiling lightly. "Want to trade?"

As if we'd rehearsed it, Alexis retrieved from his pocket Isobel's ring. He presented it to her in his outstretched palm.

Isobel let out a sob and rushed into Alexis's arms. The crowd applauded. "Thank god," Isobel said through her tears. "I knew you would finally—" Isobel stopped, too overcome to finish.

I was almost afraid to look at Nikos. It seemed that everything good in the world was hinging on his reaction.

Nikos's eyes were still fixed on Alexis. With Isobel safely in his arms, Alexis took on a strength that he conveyed to his brother without words. Maybe he was apologizing. Or expressing gratitude. Maybe both. Nikos finally turned his eyes on me, and my heart began to pound. I forced myself to remain conscious, upright, and calm.

He stepped toward me and instantly I knew everything would be all right. He'd hold me to him. All would be forgiven, with every lover in his rightful place. Just as it was in Bollywood, Nikos would finally see me as his perfect mate because, after all, nothing stands in the way true love.

But Nikos kept walking. He brushed past me, up the stairs, and out of the ballroom. I stood frozen in humiliation, utterly at a loss for motor skills. I came out of my stupor long enough to look up at Alexis in sheer bafflement. He loosened his hold on Isobel.

"He's such a stubborn bastard. Always was. Give him a minute." Alexis smiled warmly. "Then go get him."

I turned toward the gaping ballroom doors.

"Wait, Norah," Isobel said. "It was you who did this?" There was genuine tenderness in her voice. "Thank you."

I bit my lip and started walking, but Alexis caught my wrist. "No crying."

There were a few party-goers lounging in the lobby but no sign of Nikos. No sign of my merry band of pals, either.

The more I searched, the angrier I got. I didn't know what to do with myself, parading around the hotel lobby like a freak with my gown hiked up so it wouldn't catch on the furniture. Was I so dense? What more did I need to get it through my head that I wasn't enough for Nikos?

"Fuck this," I said to no one. I got into the elevator and rode, seething, up to the Presidential Suite. The door was open when I got there.

Baz, Helen, and David were all crowded on the bed, talking nervously. Helen jumped up when I entered the room.

"What happened? Tell us! We couldn't see a thing, so we came up to wait for you."

"I bet Davey a box of Opaline that once Nikos saw you in that dress he'd either propose or drop dead of a coronary," said Baz. "Are you here to show us the rock or shall I call 911?"

I couldn't move. Looking at my friends sitting there anxiously waiting for me to fill them in was more than I could take. What could I say? I'd failed.

"Norah, what is it?" Helen pulled me onto the bed. I sat, stared.

"It's done," I said. "He's gone."

"What do you mean, 'gone'?" David asked.

"He took one look at Isobel and Alexis together and he left."

"That bastard," Baz said, jumping up. "I'll teach him to reject my fiancée."

"Baz, sit down," I said, taking his hand and patting it. "It's okay. I feel fine now. I was upset, but you know what? I'm not anymore. I feel really, really good. I do. Just this minute, the fog has cleared. Right now, all I really want to do is—"

Baz handed me a vase from off the nightstand. I looked at it, then at him.

"Go on," he said. "You deserve it."

I stood up slowly. From where I was standing, I could have made a nice dent in the front wall if I gave the vase a good and hearty toss. Not to mention the incredibly satisfying sound the shattering porcelain would make.

I walked over to a glass table and carefully placed the vase it in its center, atop a crocheted doily.

Baz made a small noise of disappointment, but it hardly had time to leave his lips. I grasped the edge of the table with both hands and in one great heave, I flipped the entire thing over, sending everything on top airborne.

Helen screamed with glee and ducked. But there was no satisfying shatter; the vase had hit the carpet and bounced. Everything else on the table—papers, a pen or two, an empty paper cup, and the doily—behaved similarly. We were all silent a moment, staring at the mess.

"Well, that was anti-climactic," said David.

"Feel better, Petal?"

"Oh, yeah," I said, righting the table.

Without another word, I replaced the papers, pens, cup, doily, and vase. And then I left.

On my way out the front doors of the hotel, I passed by the darkened bar. There was Nikos, his tux jacket draped over the taps. He was in the middle of pouring himself a Scotch. I went in and gingerly lowered myself onto a stool.

"Mind if I join you? It's been a rough night."

Nikos downed his drink and poured himself another. He did not offer me one, he did not look at me.

I sucked up the silent treatment as long as I could. That is to say, the length of time it took Nikos to get halfway through his second drink and light a Marlboro.

"Why are you punishing me?"

"Do you have any idea what you've done?" His voice boomed. I nearly fell off my barstool.

"Yes," I yelled back at him. "I gave your family a chance to be whole again."

"Norah, you don't know Alexis the way I do. He's just going to end up hurting her again. It wasn't some bad judgment he made. He's sick. Like our father. You think he can just magically turn off the violence?"

"Yes, I do."

"Well, you're wrong."

"How can you be so sure?"

He turned to me. "I'm his brother."

"As his brother, then, I'm sure you know why Alexis hit Isobel in the first place." Nikos looked down. "No? Because I do. Of course, I'm not his family, so what could I possibly understand about the intricate inner workings of your complex clan? Shit, I'm so self-absorbed I couldn't possibly understand anyone but myself. That's probably why I'm so bad at my job."

The muscles in Nikos's jaw started rippling.

"Look, I can't tell you why I know what people want—what they truly want—even if they don't say it outright. Call it a gift. Not that it's done a lot of good for my own happiness."

"Poor you," Nikos mumbled into his drink.

There was such meanness in his voice that I instinctively recoiled although I was sure his spite wasn't meant for me. I knew too well what it felt like to be so angry you couldn't see straight. I also knew what I had to do. I had no desire to give him the opportunity to do something he'd regret later, now that he'd already said something he surely would.

"Take care of yourself, Nikos," I said, sliding off the bar stool. This was it. I was leaving and I'd never see him again. "If you're ever in L.A.—" I stopped short, afraid my voice would crack.

"I guess you'll be listed under Vancouver by then."

"What?"

He took out his wallet and removed a folded piece of newspaper, which he tossed onto the bar before pouring another drink. I picked it up. It was the gossip rag article. By its rumpled state, it seemed he'd been carrying it around with him for quite a while.

"Yeah, well. Don't believe everything you read," I said. "Especially in anything called 'Gabby's Gab'. But speaking of big announcements, weren't you and Isobel supposed to make one tonight?"

Nikos shrugged. "I don't know now."

"Yeah, I guess I threw a fat old wrench into that, didn't I?" I headed for the door.

"That's it?"

I stopped, but didn't turn around. My weep meter was dangerously in the red. "What do you want from me, Nikos?"

"Tell me why Lex hit Isobel."

"He's your brother. Ask him yourself."

You Can Go Home Again

I walked all the way back to my apartment. Actually, first I walked, then I ran. After I'd cut across Park Avenue, I took off my T-straps and slung them over my shoulder. Barring a few vocally-appreciative studs staggering out of corner bars, no one took much notice of the gal in the red gown flat-footing it up Lexington. It was Halloween after all.

This late at night, there were no more trick-or-treaters. To anyone looking, I might have just come from a masquerade party that went badly. That wasn't too off the mark; I had spent the evening dressed as someone I wasn't, and at the end, my true identity was finally revealed.

When I hit 59th Street and First Avenue, it began to rain. I ducked under the Queensboro Bridge, looking like a Cotillion Barbie that had been dropped in the pool. It was there under that bridge, relatively sheltered from the hot rain, that I realized tomorrow I would be leaving New York. With all that was going on, the reality hadn't had a chance to sink in. Seized by a bolt of fear that I would never have enough time to say goodbye, I rushed back out into the rain and began to run up the avenue.

"Goodbye, Le Pain Quotidien!" I yelled as I passed. "Bye, Kinkos! See you, Bloomie Nails!"

It was like some twisted, reverse reenactment of *It's a Wonderful Life*. A loony woman in the rain dressed in a ruined ball gown, howling wild farewells to the home she loved. I jumped in puddles, I smacked my hands against the signposts. I shouted and hooted. It was a miracle I wasn't arrested.

By the time I got home, my hairpiece was limp, my feet black with street muck. I peeled off my dress and tossed it into the tub.

There wasn't much else to do now but towel off and get packing. Somehow, even though I'd hauled my big black dusty suitcase out from under my bed, I couldn't bring myself to fill it. I poured a glass of wine and paced around the apartment.

The suitcase's big gaping mouth remained open, hungry, but something wasn't right. I couldn't bring myself to feed it one single article of my life.

"Come on, Norah," I encouraged myself. "L.A. will be perfect for you." I marched into the living room and picked up my copy of *Devdas*. Before I could toss it into the suitcase, something stopped me. "How do I know it's going to be perfect?"

My instincts have always told me what everyone else around me needed. But had I been right about anything in my own life? I looked deep into the eyes of Devdas and Paro that were gazing dreamily out at me from the front cover.

"What should I do?" I begged them. "Give me a sign."

I waited. Counted to three. Nothing. Honestly, what did I expect? If a lightning bolt hit me or the paintings on my wall started spinning, I would have stroked out.

With a sigh, I tucked the DVD under my arm and headed back into the living room. I slid the DVD into the player and turned on the television. It felt so good to nestle into my reliable couch dent, my legs tucked up underneath me. I looked to my right, where Nikos once sat. Then I squeezed my eyes shut and shook the image from my mind.

"This is *my* couch. *My* apartment." I pulled my favorite movie-watching blanket over me with a smile. "My life."

I woke to a banging on the door. The television was off. I didn't remember turning it off.

"Yes?" I called from the couch.

"Norah, it's Helen. We're all downstairs waiting."

Still cocooned in the blanket, I opened the door. Helen was dressed in a smart cream suit. "What are you doing? It's the middle of the night."

"It's ten-thirty. What are *you* doing?"

"Can't be, it's—" I leaned back to check the clock on the DVD player. "Two-eighteen. No, wait. It's blinking two-eighteen."

"There was a power outage last night in the storm. I can't believe you slept through it. It was immense. Flooding, downed power lines..." Helen came into the living room and looked around. "Where's your stuff? C'mon, c'mon. We have to get to the airport."

I sniffed once and sat back down on the couch. Helen slumped.

"You're not going."

I shook my head. "I can't, Hel."

"Is this about Nikos?"

"It's about me. I belong here. In New York." I yawned. "Besides, I didn't get a sign."

"What sign?"

"A sign to tell me what I'm supposed to do."

"Norah, I'm sure there are plenty of signs waiting for you in L.A. Let's go."

I looked at her. "I'm not leaving, Helen."

"You have to. Baz fired his L.A. assistant this morning."

"You're joking. He got rid of The Other Woman? What a good hubby."

"Yeah, so he needs you."

"No, he doesn't." I smiled. "He has you."

Helen sat down on the couch next to me. "After six years together, you're just going to pass him off?"

"It's time. I need to be my own assistant for a while. Maybe I'll come out to visit you guys in a few months."

Helen looked as if someone had kicked her puppy. "I can't do this without you."

I went over to the bookshelf and took down my Little Black New York Resource Book. "Take this," I said to Helen. "I know it's mostly New York stuff, but there are things Baz needs here that he can't get in Los Angeles."

Helen took the book tentatively. "I know of one big one."

Baz had arranged a limo for the four of us. It looked somewhat odd parked by the rows of garbage cans in front of our building.

"You're wearing that?" Baz asked. I'd thrown on some ripped jeans and a Gold's Gym T-shirt. I stepped into the limo and sat in the free seat across from him.

"She's not coming," Helen said before I could speak.

She wedged herself next to David, the Little Black New York Resource book tucked under her arm. The image was not lost on Baz. He looked at me, panic-stricken.

"Helen is going to be great for you, Baz," I said.

"Of course she will," he managed.

"She'll call me whenever she needs to. And I hope you know that if you ever have work in New York again, I'll always—"

Baz came over to my side of the car and hugged me hard. He softened his embrace and whispered in my ear, "I can't change your mind." It was a statement more than a question.

I pulled away. There were tears in his eyes. I shook my head. Baz sniffed and let out an exaggerated sigh. "Well, then," he said, smacking his thighs. "Piss off, Petal, we have a plane to catch."

I hugged Helen and David, but David stopped me as I was getting out of the limo. "Can you wait a second?" I sat back down. "First," David said, "I wanted to say thank you for making time to help me even though you had your hands full with Baz."

"Come on, I'm not that bad," Baz said.

"Yes, you are," Helen and I said simultaneously.

"More than that," David continued, "if it wasn't for you, I wouldn't have met Helen."

He reached into his coat pocket and withdrew a small black velvet box. Helen covered her mouth with her hand and looked at me.

"Helen?" David said somberly.

"Oh, my god," said Helen. She opened her door and ran out onto the street.

"Hold that thought," I said to David, and stepped out of the car.

Helen was standing at the back of the limo, leaning on the trunk and hyperventilating. I touched her shoulder.

"Norah, shit. I can't deal."

"What are you talking about? You've been waiting for this."

"I know, but," she choked. "Now it's real."

"How do you know what's in that box? Maybe it's an L.A. bus token."

"Don't joke."

"Helen," I said, smoothing the curls out of her face. "Do you love him?"

"With everything I have."

"So get your ass back in that limo and get engaged to the second hunkiest movie star in existence." I whispered, "I had to say that just in case Baz was eavesdropping." Helen put a hand to her cheek. "You gonna be all right?"

Helen nodded. "I think so."

"Because if not you can always use our little butt-wiping trick. I know you love him, but it might take the edge off."

"Right. That'll be nice for my *Entertainment Tonight* interview. 'What were you thinking about when David popped the question?' 'Well, Nancy, I was thinking about wiping his behind.'"

We got back into the car. Baz was seated on my side now. "Everything okay?" he asked me quietly. I nodded.

David still had the box in his hand, but now he was decidedly more nervous. That is, until Helen sat down next to him and gave him a big Hollywood-style kiss.

"Best seats in the house," Baz said out of the corner of his mouth.

She took the box and opened it. Inside, was a platinum ring, topped with a sparkling and sizable princess diamond.

"Helen LoPresti, will you marry—" David began.

"You bet your sweet ass I will," Helen said, throwing her arms around him.

"Baz," said David. "I was actually going to ask if you'd marry Baz."

"I'm shy," Baz said.

"Stop it, you guys," said Helen.

"You have to let me say my line," said David. "Or the magic doesn't work." Helen released him and sat patiently, trying not to stare at the ring David had now taken out of the box and held before her. "Helen LoPresti, will you marry me?"

Tears began to roll down Helen's cheeks. I was beginning to think she'd suddenly lost the ability to speak.

"See?" said David, kissing her right on a tear streak. "That's the magic."

Helen nodded.

David slipped the ring on her finger and Baz popped open a bottle of champagne he must have been hiding. Helen looked so happy, and my heart was full for her. For all of them, going to start a new life. I only wished it didn't have to be without me. But that was what I'd wanted. Time for myself.

Now I was crying, along with everyone else, mushed into a group hug that I wanted to last forever.

"Okay!" I finally blurted, somewhere between a laugh and a sob. "Get out of here already. My god, this is disgusting."

I got out of the car and tapped on Helen's window. She rolled it down. "I guess you didn't need that dumb old Exchange after all."

Helen gasped. "I can't believe I forgot to tell you. I went online this morning to delete my profile. The Exchange doesn't exist anymore. The power outage last night destroyed the whole database." She laughed. "Now there's a sign for you, huh?"

I straightened as the car pulled away with Baz, David and Helen all waving at me from inside.

Healing the Wounded Warrior

For the next month, I did nothing but everything I wanted to do. Any whim I had, I followed. I walked everywhere, taking in the city as though I were a wide-eyed tourist. Admittedly, I did a few walk-bys of the Hotel Ursula, but I never went in. Not that I wasn't tempted.

One night I dressed up and took myself out for dinner at El Arbol. As luck would have it, I got the same waiter as the night Jason stood me up.

"Will you be expecting a guest this evening," he asked cautiously.

"Not on your life," I said, flipping the napkin over my lap.

"Very good," said the waiter, handing me the menu.

"Yes," I said as I perused the most expensive entrees, "It is."

I wasn't much in the mood for Bollywood, either. Devoting three hours to watching a man and woman struggle to come together—and then inevitably do so in a fanfare of dancing and song—suddenly seemed too ironic. Was falling in love just a big dance we were all doing after all? Was the ultimate purpose of life to find a mate and settle down and procreate? The whole endeavor now struck me as utterly bizarre.

For the first time in my life, it didn't feel like I was struggling to keep up with the rest of the class. I wasn't trying to get someone to love me. A whole world of possibility opened itself.

Of course, those possibilities were about to become severely limited if I didn't find a job before my savings ran out. But because Helen didn't want to sell her apartment, I was making a little profit subletting it for her to a Japanese businessman who made the best-smelling dinners for his friends on Friday nights.

For now, I was financially able to support my latest obsession: Me.

On one of those good-smelling Friday nights, I was curled up on my couch dent watching *Entertainment Tonight*.

"On the *ET* Cover Story tonight," said Kevin with his brilliant smile, "Nancy has an exclusive sit-down with David Astor's fiancée and former personal assistant, Helen LoPresti."

"Holy sheep dip," I said, turning up the volume.

There was a close-up of Helen's ring and the camera pulled up to reveal Helen's smiling face, peaceful and radiant, sitting in the *ET* studio.

"Is it true you weren't alone when David proposed?" Nancy asked.

"Yes, that's true," said Helen. "Basil Vancouver was there."

"Basil Vancouver was with you? Talk about a moment to remember!"

"And my best friend, Norah Pasquale. She was there, too." Helen flitted her eyes to the camera and back. I put a hand to my chest.

"Wow! Even though she and Baz called off their own engagement?"

Helen nodded, solemnly. "They're still friends."

Nancy leaned in. "I have to ask you, what was going through your mind when David popped the question?"

Helen smirked. "Well, Nancy—"

"Don't say it," I said to the television, half hoping she would.

"I was thinking...I hope I don't throw up."

Nancy laughed politely and Helen bit her lip the way she always did to keep from busting into a full-out guffaw.

It wasn't at all a surprise that my iPhone started tinkling its song. I'd changed it the week before, though, to Aretha Franklin's "Respect."

"Loser," I answered, laughing.

"Bitch," said Helen. "I guess you saw it. I was trying to calculate the time difference."

"How are you?"

"Fabulous. Tan."

"Yes, I saw that. You're becoming quite the glam queen."

"I miss you. Why can't you be here to help me with the wedding?"

"Because I'm very busy wallowing in ecstatic self-absorption."

"Baz has been totally mopey since we got here."

"I'm sure. What's the matter? Did he run out of his favorite rain forest-friendly tissues? There's an 800 number on page 116 of the Official Baz Care and Maintenance Manual."

"Actually, Baz has been very low-maintenance. Especially since he fired me."

"He *what*?"

"It's all good. Davey and I were over at his Bel Air casita for Cosmos on Sunday—"

"Listen to you."

"—and Baz said he didn't want an assistant anymore. At least not while he's not working. He really does miss you, you know. We all do."

"Me, too, hon," I said. "But I promise I'll come out for the wedding. When is it?"

"Either Christmas or New Year's Day. We haven't decided."

"You realize that if you get married on Christmas you won't get as many presents."

"New Year's it is, then. You're still my Best Woman, right?"

"Only if I can wear an ugly dress."

"So," Helen said, slowly. "Have you seen you-know-who lately?"

My stomach flipped. I wrapped my arm around my middle and squeezed. "No."

"No phone calls from him? Frantic messages admitting fault?"

"I don't think that's going to happen, Helen," I said. "But it's fine. Really. I'm having a lot of fun on my own."

"I can't see you, so I can't tell if you're lying. But if you're in the process of hugging yourself at the moment, I'd say you're full of shit."

I let go of my waist and squinted at the phone. "Wow. I trained you better than I thought."

"No, silly. I'm your best friend. It's my job to sense these things."

The next morning, I went to Gilda's for my new Saturday morning double cappuccino ritual. On my way out, I held the door for a man who was coming in. It was Robin Fox.

"Norah," he said, just as surprised as I was. "This is incredible. I was just going to call you."

"You were?" I stepped out of the way to let a couple pass by.

"Wait for me," said Robin. "I'm grabbing a coffee."

We took our drinks to Carl Schurz Park and strolled along John Finley Walk. Robin filled me in on his recent trip to Prague and the exciting new artists he'd discovered there. This was the kind of thing Nikos should be doing, I thought. Maybe he was. For all I knew, he was already back in Paris.

"I saw Daag Framjen the other day," said Robin.

"Oh, yeah?"

"You didn't tell me you knew him."

"I didn't before you introduced us," I said. "Turns out Daag and I had a mutual acquaintance."

Robin looked at me. "An acquaintance." He laughed. "You're not being completely honest with me, are you?"

"Nope." I took a sip of my coffee.

"But you don't want to talk about him."

"Nope."

"Fair enough."

We walked in silence for a while. The East River was dark and lightly rolling. A boat sped along it, toward us, and past. The trees had shifted from green to copper although the air still held the lush scent of Indian summer. I took a deep breath and held it in for a second.

"Love sucks," I said, exhaling. "If I'd known, I would have opted for the lobotomy."

"Those are the two choices, huh?" Robin weighed them in his hands. "Love. Lobotomy. I think they're about the same."

I shrugged and tossed my empty coffee cup into a garbage bin. "Sure feels like it sometimes."

"So, you're still in love."

"Remember the part where you asked if I didn't want to talk about him and I said I didn't?"

"Sorry." Robin laughed and put up a hand. "I don't want to pry. But you're the one who mentioned love."

"So I did." I sat on a bench. "Fine. What do you want to know?"

Robin sat next to me. "Is it true what they say? About The Curse of the Santos Men?"

"What curse?" I asked, startled. "What do they say?"

"I was kidding."

I laughed. "A comedian. Just what I need."

"Listen, Norah. Before you think I'm on the make or something," Robin said. "It's obvious your attentions are elsewhere. It would be an act of sheer masochism for me to ask you out."

"Thank you, Robin," I said. "That's the nicest rejection I have ever gotten."

"That said, I wonder if you'd like to go out with me this weekend."

"This *is* this weekend."

"I know. Daag's added some pieces to his show. I'd love for you to see them with me. I'm cashing in my rain check."

"I know, Robin, but—"

"We don't have to call it a date."

"What do we call it, then?"

Robin thought a moment. "How about Frank?"

"Frank's good," I said, mulling it over. "I like it. We're going out on a Frank."

"Right. I was thinking tomorrow. At two?"

The gallery was set up the same as it had been for the opening, but another room had been filled, off to the side of the main show. This room was much smaller and displayed Daag's recent wood sculptures. The pieces that hung on the walls were as thin as paper, with miniscule figures etched into them.

The larger ones were the exact opposite—large, bulky masses with simple curves. Four objects that appeared to be poles went from floor to ceiling in each corner of the room. At first I thought they were part of the gallery structure itself, but when I passed one, I saw that a face had been carved into it. I smiled in recognition that the face was Annika's.

"He finally got it down," I said, running my fingers over her brow.

"It wasn't easy," said a voice behind me.

"What's up, Daag?" I said. "I had no idea you'd be here."

"Do you like the wood pieces?"

"I do. You've done so much since—" I stopped and smiled at him.

"Have you seen Nikos yet?" asked Daag.

I caught my breath. Not noticeably, I hoped. "Is he here?"

"Over there." Daag pointed. "By the door."

The only people I saw by the door were Robin and a woman with a miniature terrier peeking out of her shoulder bag. Daag took my arm and walked me over to a pedestal that had been hidden by one of the massive poles.

I let out a little moan. There on a pedestal was a wooden bust of Nikos. The likeness was so perfect that there were characteristics of his face I'd forgotten how much I missed. The subtle groove under his cheekbone. The thin ridge around his lips. How could I have lost that? It used to mesmerize me whenever he spoke.

I wanted so badly to touch him that I forced my hands into my pockets. When I looked at Daag, he was smiling.

"I'll leave you."

"Don't," I said, too quickly. "I mean, it's okay. You don't have to."

"But I do," said Daag. "I have a phone call." He took a vibrating cell phone from his pocket. He flipped it open and winked as he walked away.

No one was around. I made sure of that.

Then I kissed Nikos. His lips were hard and cool, but the fullness of them was there. It was easy to remember their softness and how perfectly they fit between my own. Flushed, I pulled back and looked around again, this time for Robin.

I found him in the main part of the gallery, watching the video display.

"Hey, Robin," I said. "I'm going to go."

"You sure? I was going to ask Daag for lunch. I thought you might like to join us."

"No, but thanks. For everything." I kissed his cheek. "This was the best Frank I've ever had."

Foggy-headed, I stepped out onto the sidewalk, hands returned to the depth of my pockets. Crap. Kiss one dumb statue and now I have to start my Nikos detox all over again.

The depression, I anticipated, would hit me about five minutes after I got to my empty apartment and realized I couldn't go crawling to Helen for a pep talk. My cure-all Bollywood diversion was out. I wasn't about to start smoking again. And there was no point in getting angry and throwing things, either; I'd been calm and sober for nearly a month now. I was going to have to find a new pick-me-up, and fast.

All wound up in my new predicament, I stepped onto Hudson Street without looking. Out of nowhere, a car screeched to a halt, only inches from flattening my toes. I lost my balance and fell forward onto the hood.

"Jesus Christ," I yelled, petrified.

I took a step back. Silver Mercedes. The passenger side window eased down. I swallowed hard and looked in, right at Nikos. He was smiling at me.

"Need a ride, little girl?"

I braced myself against the doorframe. His hair had grown longer, but other than that, not much seemed different about him. "How did you know I'd be—"

Nikos unlatched the passenger side door and I slid in. "You think you're the only one who knows what people want?" he asked, pulling back into traffic. "Looks like Daag's got talent in that department, too."

"He called you?"

"No, I called him to finalize some business. He told me you were there at the gallery—"

"Oh."

"—making out with my sculpture."

I snapped my head toward Nikos. He was regarding me over the tops of his sunglasses, taking entirely too much pleasure in my now very obvious mortification.

"That's really sick, Norah."

"Shut up, Nikos," I said, staring out the window. But acting indignant was too absurd. I started laughing and couldn't say another word until we pulled up to the Hotel Ursula.

"What are we doing here?" I asked as we got out.

"I have to pick up some things." Nikos held the front door open for me. "And there's something I want to show you."

Several incredibly pertinent questions ran through my mind as we rode the elevator up to the penthouse. Most importantly, I was dying to know what happened with Isobel and Alexis. Not to mention Isobel and Nikos. Was he going back to Paris? Were they all? What would happen to the hotel?

And then there was the matter of Nikos's attire. Now that the shock had, for the most part, worn off and I had regained some semblance of cogency, I noted that Nikos was not dressed in his usual crisp fashion. He wore a blue, slightly fraying workshirt over a paint-spattered T-shirt, brown work boots that bore matching paint spatters, and—yes, indeedy—a pair of khaki chinos that fit his backside like a dream.

"Wow," I said.

"What?" he asked, pulling open the elevator gate.

"Your get-up. You look so comfortable."

Nikos smiled. "You have no idea."

He unlocked the penthouse and let me in. It was incredible. Like something out of a modern architecture magazine. All cool colors and flat surfaces.

"Have a seat, if you can find one," he said.

There were packing boxes lining the walls and stacked in corners. I ran my hand over one of them.

"You're leaving?"

"Yeah," said Nikos, zipping a few coats into a wardrobe bag.

I lifted the edge of a drop cloth, peered at a crushed velvet couch. "When?"

"Now," said Nikos, dropping a couple of bags at the front door.

I went clammy. Maybe Devdas had the right idea. I should adopt heavy drinking as my new lifestyle choice. Starting as soon as I got back to my apartment. Maybe even before.

"But first, do me a favor," said Nikos. "See that print on the wall?" He pointed to a large photograph of the Acropolis in a brushed pewter frame. "Take it down for me."

I crossed the room and lifted the print. Underneath it, there was a hole in the wall plaster, about the size of a softball.

"And that one," said Nikos, pointing to a painting of a snowy forest on the adjoining wall. I did as he said, and found another hole underneath, this one larger than the first.

I turned to Nikos for an explanation, but he was in the process of taking down two framed diplomas, each with similar holes underneath them.

"Man," I said. "You either have a serious rodent problem or—" I spun around slowly, surveying all the damage. "Oh, my god, Nikos. You're a closet rager!"

He smirked and gave a modest bow. "This one was my last," he said, indicating one of the two he'd just uncovered, which also happened to be the biggest hole of all. "I did it the night of the party. After you left."

I stood there, blinking. Nikos didn't speak either. He just looked at me sadly.

"I don't know where to start," he said, finally. "I was so hard on you for playing games, not being honest, letting your anger get the best of you. And all along it was myself I was talking to. I've been a shit and I'm sorry."

When I still said nothing, Nikos sighed.

"I asked Alexis why he hit Isobel. He told me. And about how terrible he felt. See, Norah, you were right. If you hadn't brought my brother here, he and I may never have spoken to each other again. And if my mother ever thought that after she died—"

Nikos stopped and then smiled faintly. "I wish you could have met her. She was so funny. In a quirky way. And beautiful." He laughed. "In a quirky way."

"I have trouble picturing anyone in your blood line being quirkily beautiful," I said.

"Do you want to see her picture?"

I nodded. "But I warn you, if she looks anything like me I'll be forced to run screaming from this room and directly into therapy."

Nikos opened the box next to him and withdrew a small frame. Then he looked at me and spoke the two most erotic words a man can say to a woman who adores him.

"Come here."

I went to him, but I did not take the picture. I slipped between his legs, took his face in my hands, and kissed him. When I pulled back, I turned my head toward the photo he held.

His mother was indeed beautiful. Dark-haired, just like her sons. She was sitting in a beach chair wearing a 1960s Hollywood starlet-style one-piece bathing suit, shielding her eyes from the sun. Her long legs were crossed and angled off to the side with the innate glamour women back then seemed to possess. There was no question Ursula was glamorous. Even with her tongue sticking out.

You Can Go Home Again (Take 2)

It appeared I was being kidnapped for the second time. Nikos wouldn't tell me where we were going or where he was eventually heading, except to say he was leaving the hotel business. In fact, that had been his and Isobel's big announcement on the night of the party.

Their original plan was that he would still own Hotel Ursula, but Isobel would take over its management, and her protégée Claire would run the Millennium Conference Center, leaving Nikos to return to his art dealing.

But now that Alexis was back in the picture, he and Isobel decided to split their time together between New York and Paris, so that the hotels would be covered and she could spend time in her home city.

"But if they're taking the penthouse, where will you live?" I asked this several times in one form or another as Nikos drove along the parkway. He put me off as long as he could, but soon the answer was apparent. In fact, I kept my mouth shut for the last fifteen minutes of the ride, piecing it all together.

We pulled into the drive of Daag's guesthouse just as the sun was setting. I hadn't brought so much as a toothbrush, but I didn't care. Seeing that incredible place again overshadowed any thought I could have had about personal hygiene.

"This is your new home, I take it," I said as we walked up the gravel drive.

Nikos was still silent. I stepped up to the front door and he let us in. A fire was already going in the living room fireplace.

"Is Daag here?" I asked.

Nikos nodded. Just then, we both heard the back screen door shut. "But not anymore," said Nikos.

I squinted at him. "Something's going on. What is it?"

He headed up the spiral staircase.

"Wait," I said. "I mean, believe me, I am dying to go up there right about now, but something feels off."

Nikos leaned on the railing and sighed. Then he came back downstairs took my hands. "You want something off? That can be arranged. Follow me."

When we reached the bedroom, I gasped. The room was awash in candlelight. Wildflowers were everywhere—in vases, buckets, drinking glasses. Stalks of goldenrod and Queen Anne's Lace were even strewn across the bed.

Nikos gently lay me on the bed, among the flowers.

"This."

He kissed me lightly on the forehead.

"Is just to say."

He kissed me once on each cheek.

"Thank you."

Nikos placed his lips against mine. They opened. Just enough to let him in. I wrapped my arms around his neck and drew him down to me. All of it had come to this, my chance finally to let him into my heart, my body, without fear or reservation.

"And this," I said, sliding out from under him and pressing him back on the bed, "is just to say how very welcome you are."

I straddled his solid hips and began to undress him slowly. My luxurious pace was not so much for his sensual pleasure as my own. Here was this unbelievable gift I was unwrapping. It was like nothing I had ever experienced.

Nikos seemed to be enjoying my selfish pleasure, doing little to help me but lifting an occasional arm or leg to help ease his clothing off. He watched me intently, but I couldn't keep eye contact. There was too much to take in. A great feast was spread before me and I was starving for all of it at once. I felt his eyes on me, though. The strongest aphrodisiac of all.

I stepped off the bed to remove my clothes. Nikos's hands were folded under his head as he waited and watched. He was such an incredible vision that I nearly forgot how to work the button on my jeans. Naked, I crawled back down to Nikos and devoured him whole. I made love to every inch of his body with my lips, tongue, fingertips. Everything I had I gave to him. All of it.

All of me.

We went down to the kitchen in the darkness and Nikos lit a couple of candles on the table. He'd thrown his workshirt and boxers back on. I pulled on my shirt, but nothing else. The muscles in my legs and arms held a vibrant ache.

Nikos poured two glasses of wine, then took something out of a drawer, which I couldn't see in the dark. He sat down at the table and lifted his glass.

"Wow," he said.

"I'll drink to that." I leaned back and pulled my legs up to my chest. "I love this house."

"I love you," Nikos said.

This was the point I knew I was supposed to say I loved him too, but I was completely spellbound by the words coming from him, to me. I'm sure the look on my face was enough of a reciprocation; Nikos was smiling.

"I'm glad you like it here," Nikos said, placing a small box on the table in front of me. It was a red satin box with two tiny golden hinges at its back. A kind of ring-sized box.

I straightened. "What is that?"

"Open it."

"Nikos," I started, stopped. I tried again, "If this is... I mean, I don't know if... It's just that—"

Nikos laughed and pushed the box toward me. "Shush. Open it."

Gingerly, I lifted the box and unhinged it. It was a ring box, all right, only there was no ring wedged between the two velvet pillows inside. There was a shiny, brass key. Nikos took the box, removed the key, and it held up in front of me. "This is yours," he said.

"You're giving me a key."

Nikos placed the key in my palm. "I'm giving you this house." He curled my fingers around the key and held his hands over mine. "I just bought it from Daag."

"You bought me a house." I sounded like a zombie.

"However," said Nikos, sipping his wine, "I come with it."

"Like a cabana boy?"

"Something like that."

The reality hit me. "But my apartment! I can't give it up."

"Who's asking you to?"

"Nikos," I said.

"Yes?"

"I love you."

"I know."

This was the first New Year's Day I'd ever spent sweating. Ten in the morning and already seventy-five degrees. Baz, David, and Nikos were off doing something breakfast-related, but Helen and I chose to stay back and lounge. We sat on Baz's back terrace, watching the wedding planner orchestrate the crew in setting up chairs on the lawn. Considering she was getting married in seven hours, Helen seemed remarkably calm.

"It's just going to be us and a few work pals," said Helen, sipping a mimosa.

"You didn't want a big wedding anyway," I said.

"Sure I did. When I was eighteen. Now I don't care. I'm happy to be getting married before my tits fall down to my ankles."

"Lovely image to put in my head before I've had coffee."

"Let's see. Dress is ready. Food is coming. Flowers, too. Tuxes aren't my responsibility. Table's set. Band's confirmed." Helen sighed. "Nothing left to do but start getting nervous."

"Are you?"

"Right now I just feel like I've been planning a party. I guess it hasn't sunk in yet that it's in my honor." Helen smiled and settled into the warmth of the sun. She rolled her head toward me and opened one eye. "How are things with Nikos?"

"Great. He's putting his first show together. All the artists are immigrants who live and work in New York. I've been helping get everyone ready for the show, doing paperwork. I had to do some serious schmoozing to get this Palestinian artist's visa extended—"

"You're an assistant again."

"I guess it's in the blood."

Helen was quiet a moment. "Do you think you'll marry him?"

"No idea."

"Do you want to?"

Two men on ladders draped a string of white roses over the gazebo. "That's what it's supposed to come to, I guess."

"Stop, you're killing me with the romance."

"I don't know, Helen. I don't have a problem with marriage. But like you just said, you feel like you've been planning a party and that's about it. Well, that's how I feel about the idea of marriage. You have a big party, but it doesn't change much."

Helen sat up. "Oh, yes it does. And it should. Look, I love David. If we couldn't get married for some reason, I'd still love him. But the ritual is very important, Norah. It is a rite of passage that says you take your love seriously."

"Why can't just being with him say that?"

"It does. But a wedding is like, I don't know, like hairspray on a fabulous 'do. It fixes it in place."

"Until it rains."

"Don't pick on my analogy. You know what I'm saying."

"I do. I just think the whole process is so tired. You have to keep up with the dating-mating dance until you get him to take the leap and buy you a ring."

"Norah, do you have any doubt that Nikos is the man you want to spend the rest of your life with?"

"None."

"Do you think he feels the same way?"

"Please, Helen. The man bought me an entire house."

Helen leaned back in her chair and sipped her drink. "So, why wait for him?"

"Are you suggesting that I propose to Nikos?"

"Why not? Stir up tradition."

I sat up, suddenly inspired. "I'll buy *him* a ring."

"Now you're cooking," said Helen, picking a bit of orange pulp from between her teeth with a manicured pinky nail. "I'll help you pick it out. We'll go to my favorite jeweler. She's a hoot."

"Don't you have enough to do today?"

"Nope," said Helen, getting up. "I'm off duty for the next few hours. Besides, it'll be good for me. Keep me from freaking out. But you have to drive. I just drank my breakfast."

Helen directed me east, through Hollywood, to a bungalow in Echo Park. We got out of the car and maneuvered our way through a yard full of kids' toys to the front door.

"You'll love Kenne," Helen said, ringing the doorbell.

The woman who came to the door looked to be forty or so. Her skin was the color of caramel, off-setting a wild mane of kinky blond hair. There were freckles dotting her nose and cheeks. She wore jeans, a Monty Python T-shirt, and a purple cape.

"Helen!" she said and kissed both her cheeks. "I'm so glad you called. Everything's in the studio. Come on in."

"Kenne, this is Norah," said Helen as we headed through the house to the back. We passed two kids in the living room, a boy and a girl, wearing matching green capes and holding yellow foam swords.

"Good to know you, Norah. That's Henry and June." Kenne turned back and rolled her eyes. "I know, I take a lot of heat for it, but they're family names. What're you gonna do?" They waved at us. "Hold the fort, kids." Henry and June started bashing each other with the foam swords.

Laid out on a table in the studio were about forty bands in silver and gold. Each had individual markings and layers. No two were alike.

"If you see any designs here you like, I can recast them in any metal you want," said Kenne.

"They're all incredible," I said.

"Helen said this is for a man friend of yours?"

"Yeah," I said absently, lifting a silver-colored band with watery markings on it.

"Like that one? I've been working in platinum lately. The stains are a light acid wash."

"Nice effect," said Helen. "You didn't have this when David and I were picking out our bands."

Kenne shook her head. "It's an experiment."

"Well, so is this," I said, making Kenne laugh. "But I don't know his size," I said.

"How tall is he?"

I raised a hand in the air about eight inches above my head.

"Let's call it six-two. He's probably about a ten or eleven, then. That one's ten-and-a-half. But it's no problem," said Kenne. "If you like it, I can make it a perfect fit."

I couldn't take my eyes off the ring. Every time I turned it over in my hands, its design seemed to catch light and shift. When I eventually looked up, Helen was smiling.

"Norah, I think that's the one."

I handed the ring back to Kenne. "I'll take it."

When we got back to Baz's I stuffed the ring deep into my suitcase. I didn't know when I would give it to Nikos, or if I really planned to. But I liked having it.

I even thought about it during Helen's and David's wedding as I stood by Helen's side, catching glances at Nikos sitting a few feet away, imagining him standing next to me as my groom. At the reception, Helen handed me her bouquet instead of tossing it.

"Just helping fate along," she said.

After the guests left, the four of us kept the party going until it was dark. Baz refused to take off his tux even after we'd all switched into bathing suits for a midnight swim, rationalizing that he looked "far too fabulous."

I'd had my dip and was enjoying a glass of champagne with Baz and Nikos on the terrace. Helen and David were making out in the pool.

"I wish we didn't have to go back tomorrow," I said. "I miss these times. You and me getting drunk, Helen and David going at each other."

"That's right, you have your first opening, Nikky," Baz said. "That's exciting, isn't it? You should be very proud, you two."

"It's this weekend already," said Nikos, tracing the nape of my neck with his finger. "It would be great if you could come."

"Ah," said Baz. "Well, I can't because I'm working."

"You are? Doing what? Is it another show?" I asked. "Relax, Petal, it's still early days. I'm taking a meeting with the HBO folks to sign all the contracts and such, but it looks as though I'll be starring in a little biopic on the life of Walt Whitman."

"That's fantastic," said Nikos.

"And of course Whitman means?" Baz asked, waiting for me to catch up.

"You finally get to play gay," I concluded.

"Whitman." Nikos poked me in the ribs. "New York."

"Bingo, stud," said Baz. "And working in New York means I'll be needing a—oh, what do you call those things? Ah, yes. A wife."

"Oh, Basil!" I jumped out of my seat and hopped in his lap, still wet from the pool. "I do!"

Baz laughed and kissed me. I turned to Nikos, my arms still around Baz's neck. "This must look very strange."

"I have no words to describe."

"Not to worry, mate," said Baz. "Ours is a strictly business type of total adoration."

"I feel much better," said Nikos.

Baz smacked my thigh. "All right, Petal, up you get. I'm all wet."

"Behave," I said, standing.

"The suit," he said, raising his eyebrow at me. "Attention Mr. and Mrs. Helen LoPresti," he yelled to the love birds in the pool, "Get off each other and let's eat some fucking cake."

No one was prepared for the success that came with Nikos's opening. Sure, there had been press about the hotel heir turning to the art world, but for those of us in on the actual nitty gritty of the project, the show was simply a collection of new work that needed to be seen.

No small feat, true. And the work was superior. Nikos called the show "Mondo Manhattan." Each piece the international artists created was inspired by their experiences immigrating to and living in New York City. Daag had a new wood sculpture in it: intricately carved limbs from a tree he loved in Central Park that had been badly damaged during Hurricane Sandy. Robin Fox gave a stunning review in *The New York Times* that kept the 57th Street gallery packed for the duration of the show.

Nikos and I threw a big party at the house on the night the show closed in March. Isobel and Alexis came, too. I hadn't seen much of them since the night of the Hotel Ursula bash; they spent more time in Paris than they'd planned.

If I had any doubts about bringing the two of them back together, they were quelled when I saw them at the house, laughing and talking and mingling as though they'd never been apart. Even Nikos commented on their happiness as I refilled the ice bucket in the kitchen.

As I dropped scoops of ice into the bucket, it occurred to me that Nikos and I were truly a couple now. People referred to us as a unit: "What are you and Nikos doing this summer?" "Nikos and Norah redid the patio themselves." "Did you ask Norah and Nikos about how they met? It's hysterical."

Sometimes that old monkey of low self-esteem still took nostalgic rides on my back no matter how much Nikos told me he loved me, no matter how well we worked and lived together. Maybe that was why I still hadn't taken the ring I bought him out of my suitcase since the day I bought it. But it came with me in that same suitcase every weekend I went to spend with him at our house.

That's not to say there hadn't been moments—quite a few of them—that I thought very seriously about giving Nikos the ring. After a good dinner or a walk in the woods. One night, we even watched the special edition, marathon-length DVD of *Lord of the Rings* together, curled up on the couch in each other's arms.

"That's some ring, huh?" I said as the credits rolled.

"Sure is."

"What would you do if someone gave you a ring like that?"

Stupid. Transparent. If I thought it would fit, I would have stuck my entire foot in my mouth, straight up to the ankle. Nikos looked down at me curiously, burrowing as I was now in the crook of his armpit, trying to hide my shame. He picked up the remote and clicked over to the special feature section.

"I suppose I'd accept it."

I peered up at him, one eye still hiding behind a fold in his sweater. "Really?"

"Yes," said Nikos, flicking a piece of popcorn at my head. "I would."

You'd think with an endorsement like that—albeit couched in cryptic metaphor—that I'd have the confidence to propose to Nikos. But every time I envisioned the actual act, I could only picture Nikos saying no, that he liked everything as it was. Truth was, so did I.

What would I do then? You can't go back to your old life together after you make a gaffe like that. Hovering over you all the time is the fact that you took a giant leap and fell flat on your face.

How do men do it?

This, I swear, was the question in my mind as I brought the ice bucket back into the living room where Nikos had everyone gathered and seated. It was as though I'd walked into my own surprise birthday party but everyone had forgotten to yell surprise. All our guests were looking at me expectantly.

I lifted the bucket. "Uh, here's the ice. The party can go on." Nikos took the bucket from my hand and led me into the center of the room. And then he got down on one knee.

Oh, this man was classy. What guts. All these people here, including an ex-lover, and he's about to propose. I wished I could be like him. Out there, living life as it came, not giving a shit about the consequences.

"Norah," said Nikos.

I don't know what possessed me, but suddenly I was down on one knee as well. Everyone laughed.

"I don't think you have to do that," Nikos whispered.

"Are you going to propose?" I whispered back.

"That was the idea, yes."

"Wait!" I bolted upstairs.

I could hear the rumblings of the guests as I rummaged around in my suitcase. I grabbed the ring and was about to shove it in my pocket when I turned around to see Nikos standing in the doorway.

"If this is a bad time—" said Nikos.

"I have something to say first. Can I?"

Nikos rolled back against the doorway and crossed his arms over his chest. "Sure."

I took the ring from my pocket and gave it a squeeze for good luck. "Nikos, will you marry me?"

I unfolded my hand, exposing the ring. I held fast, looking Nikos directly in his eyes, hoping to all that was good in the world that I wasn't going to regret this.

Nikos stared at me in total shock. He glanced at the ring. Still, he said nothing.

"Say yes," I whispered, and he looked back at me. "Nikos, please. Say something."

"Do you have to control everything?"

"What? What do you mean? Why can't I give you a ring?"

"Because I wanted to give you one. On my own. Without competition." Nikos squared off, blocking the doorway, which I now very much wanted to bolt through. "There's a room full of people down there I was prepared to make a fool of myself in front of in order to give you a gift. Make a commitment to you. Why can't you accept that?"

"It feels weird," I said. "I'm used to being The One, you know? The orchestrator."

"Well, you're not now." Nikos said testily. Then he softened. "Are you okay with that?"

"This is how it's going to be with us, huh?" I asked. "We're going to butt heads."

"Probably. A lot."

I thought a moment. Not about anything heavy. Mainly seasons passing. The Forsythia blooming on the trees lining the woods behind the house. The lilacs along the drive. The crisping of warm winds as fall comes near. Snow. Shoveling. Fires in the fireplace. The braided rugs being hung outdoors and slapped free of dust and discarded particles of life. Our lives. Together.

"Nikos?"

"Yes."

"Will you marry me?"

"Yes," said Nikos, as though it were the most obvious thing in the world. It was when I took his hand and slipped the ring on his finger that the tears of relief came. It was a perfect fit.

Just like a film. But better.

"Now let's go downstairs," he said. "It's my turn."

The Little Mrs.

I stood at Baz's arrival gate in JFK holding up a white placard that read: BLEU, for old time's sake.

Weary cross-country travelers filed out of the doors. I watched them for a while, trying to spot Baz, but I was constantly distracted by the engagement ring on my finger.

Finally, Baz emerged. He was easy to spot. Not only did he look fresh as a daisy, but he was the only person signing autographs with one hand while simultaneously dragging a carry-on with the other.

"Pardon me," I said as I dropped the placard and made my way through the crowd. Camera bulbs had suddenly begun flashing so much that I feared they'd set off epileptic seizures. "Baz," I called out. "*Basil!*"

Baz peered over the sea of people and pushed on, a big smile on his face. As the throng encircled us, Baz slipped off his sunglasses, took me in his arms and laid on me the longest, wettest, Hollywood kiss ever performed for a live audience.

I went along with it, wrapping my arms around him.

"Look at that rock!" someone yelled, and the flashbulbs went crazy again.

Baz pulled back and took my hand to regard the ring. He clucked his tongue. "I thought they were talking about my arse."

I put my arm around his waist as we headed for the doors. "We'll be reading about this in the papers tomorrow."

"Baz and Norah together again," said Baz with a dramatic sigh.

"Do you have any baggage, Mr. Vancouver?"

"Loads, Petal," said Baz as we stepped out to the waiting limousine. "But you're worlds better than therapy."

About the Author

Rachel Astarte is a transformational life coach, author, and educator. She is the author of *101 Better Sex Tips*, *The Bride of Manhattan,* and *Celebrating Solitude.* She lives in New York with her husband and son.

www.ingramcontent.com/pod-product-compliance
Lightning Source LLC
Chambersburg PA
CBHW050555260626
47157CB00002B/568